W9-COM-744

WINDOWS
ON THE
WORLD

WINDOWS ON THE WORLD

A NOVEL

FRÉDÉRIC BEIGBEDER

Translated from the French by Frank Wynne

miramax books

HYPERION

NEW YORK

This book is a work of fiction. Names, characters, businesses, organization, places, events, and incidents either are products of the author's imagination or are used fictitiously.

Printed in the United States of America. For information address Hyperion, 77 West 66th Street, New York, NY 10023-6298

ISBN 1-4013-5223-5

First Edition
10 9 8 7 6 5 4 3 2 1

"And thou, thy Emblem, waving over all!
Delicate beauty! a word to thee, (it may be salutary;)
Remember, thou hast not always been, as here to-day, so comfortably ensovereign'd;
In other scenes than these have I observ'd thee, flag;
Not quite so trim and whole, and freshly blooming, in folds of stainless silk;
But I have seen thee, bunting, to tatters torn, upon thy splinter'd staff,
Or clutch'd to some young color-bearer's breast, with desperate hands,
Savagely struggled for, for life or death—fought over long,
'Mid cannon's thunder-crash, and many a curse, and groan and yell and rifle-volleys cracking sharp,
And moving masses, as wild demons surging—and lives as nothing risk'd,
For thy mere remnant, grimed with dirt and smoke, and sopp'd in blood;
For sake of that, my beauty—and that thou might'st dally, as now, secure up there,
Many a good man have I seen go under."

Walt Whitman, *Leaves of Grass,* September 7, 1871

KILL THE ROCKEFELLERS!

Kurt Cobain, *Diaries,* 2002

Pardon me, Chloë
For having led you
Onto this devastated land

To the 2,749

Lightning Rods:

"A novelist who does not write realistic novels understands nothing of the world in which we live."

Tom Wolfe

"The function of the artist is to plunge into the depths of hell."

Marilyn Manson

8:30

YOU KNOW HOW IT ENDS: EVERYBODY DIES. DEATH, OF COURSE, comes to most people one day or another. The novelty of this story is that everyone dies at the same time in the same place. Does death forge bonds between people? It would not appear so: they do not speak to each other. They brood, like all those who got up too early and are munching their breakfast in a lavish cafeteria. From time to time, some take photos of the view, the most beautiful view in the world. Behind the square buildings, the sea is round; the slipstreams of the boats carve out geometric shapes. Even the seagulls do not come this high. The customers in Windows on the World are strangers to one another for the most part. When, inadvertently, their eyes meet, they clear their throats and bury their noses in their newspapers PDQ. Early September, early morning, everyone is in a bad mood: the holidays are over, all that's left to do is wait it out until Thanksgiving. The sky is blue, but no one is enjoying it.

In Windows on the World a moment from now, a large Puerto Rican woman will start to scream. A suited executive's mouth will fall open. "Oh my God!" Office workers will be stunned into silence. A redhead will scream, "Holy shit!" A waitress will keep pouring her tea until the cup overflows. Some seconds are longer than others, as though someone has pressed "Pause" on a DVD player. In a moment, time will become elastic. All of these people will finally get to know one another. In a moment, they will all be horsemen of the Apocalypse, all united in the End of the World.

8:31

THAT MORNING, WE WERE AT THE TOP OF THE WORLD, AND I WAS the center of the universe.

It's half past eight. Okay—it's a bit early to drag your kids up a skyscraper. But the kids really wanted to have breakfast here, and I just can't say no to them: I feel guilty about splitting up with their mother. The advantage of getting here early is that you don't have to stand in line. Since the 1993 bombing, security controls on the ground floor have been tripled; you need special badges to work here, and the security guards who search your bags don't fuck around. Even the buckle on Jerry's Harry Potter belt set off the metal detector. In the high-tech atrium, fountains gurgle discreetly. Breakfast is by reservation only: I gave my name at the Windows on the World desk when we arrived. "Good morning, my name is Carthew Yorston." Immediately you get a sense of the place: red carpet, tasseled velvet rope, private elevator. In this vast airport lounge (350 square feet under glass), the reservation desk is like a First Class check-in. It was a brilliant idea to show up early. The lines for the telescopes are shorter (pop a quarter in and you can stare at the secretaries arriving for work in the neighboring buildings: cell phones glued to their ears, dressed in pale gray figure-hugging pantsuits, coiffured hair, expensive sneakers, pumps stuffed into their fake Prada handbags). This is the first time I've been to the top of the World Trade Center: my sons both loved the Skylobbies—the high-speed elevators, which ascend the first 78 floors in 43 seconds. They're so fast you can feel your heart leap in your chest. They didn't want to leave the Skylobby. Finally, after four round trips, I was annoyed.

"Okay, now, that's enough! These elevators are for people going to work, it's not marked Space Mountain!"

One of the restaurant hostesses, identifiable by her lapel badge, escorted us to the other elevator, which whisks you to the 107th floor. We have a busy schedule today: breakfast at Windows on the World, then a walk in Battery Park, where we'll catch the Staten Island ferry to have a look at the Statue of Liberty, later a visit to Pier 17, a bit of shopping at South Street Seaport, some photos of the Brooklyn Bridge, a tour of the fish market just for the smell of it, and finally a medium-rare hamburger at the Bridge Café. The boys love big juicy hamburgers smothered in ketchup and large Cokes full of crushed ice—as long as they're not Diet. Kids think of nothing but food, parents of nothing but fucking. Things are pretty good on that score, thanks: shortly after my divorce, I met Candace, who works at Elite New York. You know the type . . . She makes J. Lo look like a bag lady. Every night she comes to the Algonquin and climbs all over me, moaning she prefers Philippe Starck's Royalton, which is just down the block it's because she's never read Dorothy Parker) (remember to give her a copy of *The Collected Dorothy Parker*, that'll put her off relationships.)

In two hours I'll be dead; in a way, I am dead already.

8:32

We know very little of what happened in Windows on the World that morning. *The New York Times* reports that at 8:46 A.M., the time at which American Airlines Flight 11 flew into floors 94 to 98, there were 171 people in the top floor restaurant, 72 of whom were employees. We know that the Risk Water Group had organized a working breakfast in a private dining room on 106, but also that, as they did every morning, a variety of customers were having breakfast on 107. We know that the North Tower (the higher of the two, crowned with the antenna, which made it look like a hypodermic syringe) was the first to be hit and the last to fall, at 10:28 A.M. precisely. There is therefore a time lag of exactly an hour and three quarters. Hell lasts an hour and three quarters. As does this book.

I am in Le Ciel de Paris as I write these words. That's the name of the restaurant on the 56th floor of the Tour Montparnasse, 33 avenue du Maine, 75015 Paris. Telephone: +33 1 40 64 77 64. Fax: +33 1 43 22 58 43. Métro station: Montparnasse-

Bienvenue. They serve breakfast from 8:30 A.M. For weeks now I've been having my morning coffee here every day. From here you can look at the Eiffel Tower eye to eye. The view is magnificent, since it's the only place in Paris from which you can't see the Tour Montparnasse. Around me, businessmen shout into their cell phones so their neighbors can eavesdrop on their brainless conversations:

"Listen, I can't babysit this anymore, it was actioned at the last meeting."

"No, no, I'm telling you Jean-Philippe was crystal clear, it's not negotiable."

"Look, the stock's printing on the 'O.'"

"Look, take it from me, sometimes you melt and you don't even cover your nut."

"Well, you know what they say: Rockefeller made his fortune always buying too late and selling too early."

"OK, we don't want to get whacked on this. I'll get my secretary to snail you a hard copy and we'll nail it down."

"Like a shot, the value split."

"I'll tell you something, if those assholes don't shore this fucker up, the stock is going to tank."

"I was tracking the CAC 40, but everything started crunching through the price level, and I got jigged out."

They also misuse the adverb "absolutely." As I jot down the musings of these apprentice Masters of the Universe, a waitress brings me croissants, a *café-crème*, some individual pots of Bonne Maman jam, and a couple of boiled eggs. I don't remember how the waitresses in Windows on the World were dressed: it was dark the first—and last—time I set foot in it. They probably employed blacks, students, out-of-work actresses, or maybe pretty little New Jersey girls with starched aprons. Careful: Windows on the World wasn't Mickey D's; it was a first-class joint with prices to prove it (Brunch $35, service not included). Tel: 212-938-1111 or 212-524-7000. Reservations recommended some time in advance. Jacket required. I've tried calling the number; nowadays it goes to an answering machine for some company specializing in event management. The waitresses must have been pretty, I suppose, the uniform sophisticated: a beige outfit embroidered with the initials "WW"? Or maybe they were dressed like old-fashioned chambermaids, with those little black dresses you just want to lift up? A pantsuit? A Gucci tux designed by Tom Ford? It's impossible to go back and check now. Writing this hyperrealist novel is made more difficult by reality itself. Since September 11, 2001, reality has not only outstripped fiction, it's destroying it. It's impossible to write about this subject, and yet impossible to write about anything else. Nothing else touches us.

Beyond the windows, my eyes are drawn to every passing plane. For me to be able to describe what took place on the far side of the Atlantic, a plane would have to crash into this black tower beneath my feet. I'd feel the building rock; it must be a strange sensation. Something as solid as a skyscraper rocking like a drunken boat. So much glass and steel transformed in an instant into a wisp of straw. Wilted stone. This is one of the lessons of the World Trade Center: that the immovable is movable. What we thought was fixed is shifting. What we thought solid is liquid. Towers are mobile, and skyscrapers first and foremost scrape the ground. How could something so enormous be so quickly destroyed? That is the subject of this book: the collapse of a house of credit cards. If a Boeing were to crash below my feet, I would finally know what it is that has tortured me for a year now: the black smoke seeping from the floor, the heat melting the walls, the exploded windows, the asphyxiation, the panic, the suicides, the headlong stampede to stairwells already in flames, the tears and the screams, the desperate phone calls. This does not mean that I do not breathe a sigh of relief as I watch each plane fly off into the white sky. But it happened. This thing happened, and it is impossible to relate.

Windows on the World. My first impression is that the name is slightly pretentious. A little self-indulgent, especially for a skyscraper that houses stockbrokers, banks, and financial markets. It's possible to see the words as one more proof of American condescension: "This building overlooks the nerve center of world capitalism and cordially suggests you go fuck yourselves." In fact, it was a pun on the name of the World Trade Center. Windows on the "World." As usual, with my traditional French sullenness I see arrogance where there was nothing but a lucid irony. What would I have called a restaurant at the top of the World Trade Center? "Roof of the World"? "Top of the World"? Both are worse. They stink. Why not "King of the World," like Leonardo Di Caprio in *Titanic*, while we're at it? ("The World Trade Center is our *Titanic*" declared the mayor of New York, Rudy Giuliani, on the morning after the attack.) Of course, in hindsight, the ex–ad exec in me hardly misses a beat: *there* would have been a great name for the place, the perfect brand, unassuming yet poetic: "END OF THE WORLD." "End" meaning not only the culmination, but also the farthest point. Since the restaurant was on the roof, "End of the World" could simply mean "at the top of the North Tower." But Americans don't like that kind of humor; they're very superstitious. That's why their buildings never have a thirteenth floor. All things considered, "Windows on the World" was a very appropriate name. And a very effective slogan—why otherwise would Bill Gates have chosen to dub his famous software "Windows" some years later? As a name, "Windows on the World" was "all that," as the kids say. It certainly wasn't the highest view in the world: the summit of the World Trade Center was 1,368 feet, whereas the Petronas Towers in Kuala Lumpur rise to 1,483 feet and the Sears Tower in Chicago to 1,450. The Chinese are currently building what will be the world's tallest building in Shanghai: the Shangai World Financial Center (1,614 feet). I hope the name won't bring them bad luck. I'm very fond of the Chinese: they are the only people on earth capable of being both extremely capitalist and supremely communist.

8:33

FROM HERE, THE TAXIS LOOK LIKE YELLOW ANTS LOST IN A GRIDIRON maze. Under the watchful eyes of the Rockefeller family and the supervision of the New York Port Authority, the Twin Towers were imagined by architect Minoru Yamasaki (1912–1982) and associates with Emery Roth and Sons. Two concrete and steel towers 110 stories high. Almost 10,000,000 square feet of office space. Each tower boasts 21,800 windows and 104 elevators. forty thousand square feet of office space per floor. I know all this because it's my job in some sense. Inverted catenary of triangular cross-section measuring 54 feet at the base and 17 feet at the apex; footing, 630 feet; steel lattice columns on 39-inch centers, weight 320,000 tons (of which 13,357 tons are concrete). Cost: 400 million dollars. Winner of the Technological Innovation Prize from the National Building Museum. I would have liked to be an architect; in reality, I'm a realtor. Over 250,000 cans of paint a year to maintain; 60,000 tons of cooling capacity. Every year, more than two million tourists visit the WTC. Building work on the complex began in 1966 and lasted ten years. Critics quickly dubbed the towers "the Lego-blocks" or

"David and Nelson." I don't dislike them; I like seeing the clouds reflected in them. But there are no clouds today. The kids stuff themselves with pancakes and maple syrup. They fight over the butter. It would have been nice to have had a girl, just to know what it's like to have a tranquil child, one who's not permanently in competition with the rest of the universe. The air conditioning is freezing. I'd never get used to it. Here, in the capital of the world, in Windows on the World, a high-class clientele can contemplate the acme of all Western achievement, but they have to freeze their balls off to do it. The air conditioning makes a constant droning noise, a blanket of sound humming like a jet engine with the volume turned down; I find the lack of silence exhausting. In Texas, where I come from, we're happy to die of heatstroke. We're used to it. My family is descended from John Adams, the second president of the United States. Great-granddaddy Yorston, a man named William Harben, was the great-grandson of the man who drafted the Declaration of Independence. That's why I'm a member of the Sons of the American Revolution (acronym SAR, as in *Son Altesse Royale*). Oh yes, we've got our own aristocrats in America. I'm one of them. A lot of Americans boast of being descended from the signatories of the Declaration of Independence. It doesn't mean anything, but we feel better. Contrary to William Faulkner, the South isn't just some bunch of violent, alcoholic mental defectives. In New York, I like to ham up my Texas drawl, to say "yup," instead of "yeah." I'm every bit as much a snob as the remaining survivors of the European aristocracy. We call them "Eurotrash": the playboys down at the Au Bar, the lotharios who take pride of place in Marc de Gontaut-Biron's catalog and the photo section of *Paper* magazine. We laugh at them. We yank their chain, but we have our very own, what? American Trash? I'm a redneck, a member of the American Trashcan. But my name isn't up there with Getty and Guggenheim and Carnegie because instead of buying museums my ancestors pissed everything up the wall.

Pressing the faces up against the glass, the kids try to scare each other.

"Scaredy-cat, scaredy-cat—can't even look down with your hands behind your back."

"Wow, this is weird!"

"You're just chicken!"

I tell them that in 1974, a Frenchman called Philippe Petit, a tightrope walker, illegally stretched a cable between the Twin Towers at exactly this height and walked across in spite of the cold and the wind and the vertigo. "What's a Frenchman?" the kids ask. I explain that France is a small European country that helped America to free itself from the yoke of English oppression between 1776 and 1783 and that, to show our appreciation, our soldiers liberated them from the Nazis in 1944. (I'm simplifying, obviously, for educational purposes.)

"See over there—the Statue of Liberty? That was a gift to America from France. OK, it's a bit kitsch, but it's the thought that counts."

The kids don't give a damn, even though they're big fans of "French fries" and "French toast." Right now, I'm more interested in "French kissing" and "French letters." And *The French Connection*, with the famous car chase under the El.

Through the Windows on the World, the city stretches out like a huge checkerboard, all the right angles, the perpendicular cubes, the adjoining squares, the intersecting rectangles, the parallel lines, the network of ridges, a whole artificial geometry in gray, black, and white, the avenues taking off like flight paths, the cross streets, which look as though they've been drawn on with marker, tunnels like red brick gopher holes; from here, the smear of wet asphalt behind the cleaning trucks looks like the slime left by an aluminum slug on a piece of plywood.

8:34

I OFTEN GO AND STAND BEFORE THE MARBLE PLAQUE AT 56 RUE Jacob. All American tourists should make a pilgrimage to 56 rue Jacob, instead of having their photo taken in front of the tunnel at Pont de l'Alma in memory of Diana and Dodi. It was here, on September 3, 1783, at the Hôtel d'York, that the Treaty of Paris was signed by John Adams and Benjamin Franklin, putting an end to the War of Independence with the British. My mother lives nearby; a little farther up, hidden behind a tree, are the publishers Le Seuil. People cross the road in front of this old building without realizing that it was here, a stone's throw from the Café de Flore, that the United States of America was born. Perhaps they prefer to forget.

8:34 A.M. in Le Ciel de Paris. The luxury of skyscrapers is that they allow human beings to rise above themselves. Every skyscraper is a utopia. The age-old fantasy of man has been to build his own mountains. In building towers into the clouds, man is proving to himself that he is above nature. And that's exactly how you feel at the top of one of these rockets of concrete and aluminum, glass and steel: everything I can see belongs to me, no more traffic jams, gutters, sidewalks, I am man above the world. It is not the thrill of power, but of pride. There is nothing arrogant about it. Simply the joy of knowing that one can raise oneself higher than the tallest tree and:

You vapors, I think I have risen with you, moved away to
distant continents, and fallen down there, for reasons,
I think I have blown with you you winds;
You waters I have finger'd every shore with you,
I have run through what any river or strait of the globe has
run through,
I have taken my stand on the bases of peninsulas and on
the high embedded rocks, to cry thence:

Salut au monde!
What cities the light or warmth penetrates I penetrate those
cities myself,
All islands to which birds wing their way I wing my way myself.

Toward you all, in America's name,
I raise high the perpendicular hand, I make the signal,
To remain after me in sight forever,
For all the haunts and homes of men.

The original title of Whitman's poem is "*Salut au Monde!*" In the nineteenth century, American poets spoke French. I am writing this book because I'm sick of bigoted anti-Americanism. My favorite French philosopher is Patrick Juvet: "I Love America." Since war has been declared between France and the United States, you have to be careful to choose sides if you don't want to wind up being fleeced later.

My favorite writers are American: Walt Whitman and therefore, but in his own right, Edgar Allan Poe, Herman Melville, F. Scott Fitzgerald, Ernest Hemingway, John Fante, Jack Kerouac, Henry Miller, J. D. Salinger, Truman Capote, Charles Bukowski, Lester Bangs, Philip K. Dick, William T. Vollmann, Hunter S. Thompson, Bret Easton Ellis, Chuck Palahniuk, Philip Roth, Hubert Selby Jr., Jerome Charyn (who lives in Montparnasse), Jay McInerney (whom I met in Paris).

My favorite musicians are American: Frank Sinatra, Chuck Berry, Bob Dylan, Leonard Bernstein, Burt Bacharach, James Brown, Chet Baker, Brian Wilson, Johnny Cash, Stevie Wonder, Paul Simon, Lou Reed, Randy Newman, Michael Stipe, Billy Corgan, Kurt Cobain.

My favorite film directors are American: Howard Hawks, Orson Welles, Robert Altman, Blake Edwards, Stanley Kubrick, John Cassavetes, Martin Scorsese, Woody Allen, David Lynch, Russ Meyer, Sam Raimi, Paul Thomas Anderson, Larry Clark, David Fincher, M. Night Shyamalan.

American culture dominates the planet not for economic reasons, but because of its quality. It's too easy to ascribe its influence to political machination, to compare Disney to Hitler or Spielberg to Satan. American art is constantly renewing itself because it is profoundly rooted in real life. American artists are constantly searching for something new, but something new that speaks to us of ourselves. They know how to reconcile imagination and accessibility, originality with the desire to seduce. Molière was in it for the money, Mozart wanted to be famous: there's nothing shameful about that. American artists churn out fewer theories than their European counterparts, because they haven't got time; they're too busy with the practice.

They grab hold of the world, grapple with it, and in describing it, they transform it. American authors think of themselves as realist when in fact they're all Marxists! They're hypercritical of their own country. No democracy in the world is as contested by its own literature. American independent and underground cinema is the most subversive in the world. When they dream, American artists take the rest of the world with them, because they are more courageous, more hardworking, and because they dare to mock their own country. Many people believe that European artists have a superiority complex when it comes to their American counterparts, but they're mistaken: they have an inferiority complex. Anti-Americanism is in large part jealousy and unrequited love. Deep down, the rest of the world admires American art and resents the United States for not returning the favor. A compelling example? Bernard Pivot's reaction to James Lipton (presenter of the program *The Actors Studio*) on the last *Bouillon de Culture*. The host of the finest literary program in the history of French television seemed completely intimidated by Lipton, a pompous, toadying hack who chairs sycophantic discussions with Hollywood actors on some minor-league cable channel. Pivot, who created *Apostrophes*, a man who has interviewed the finest writers of his generation, couldn't get over the fact that he was quoted in the States by a sycophantic creep.

What bothers us is not American imperialism, but American chauvinism, its cultural isolation, its complete lack of any curiosity about foreign work (except in New York and San Francisco). France has the same relationship with the United States nowadays as do the provinces with Paris: a combination of admiration and contempt, a longing to be part of it and a pride at resisting. We want to know everything about them so that we can shrug our shoulders with a condescending air. We want to know the latest trends, the places to be seen, all the New York gossip so that we can emphasize how rooted we are in the profound reality of our own country. Americans seem to have made the opposite journey to that of Europe: their inferiority complex (being a nouveau riche, adolescent country whose history and culture have, for the most part, been imported) has developed into a superiority complex (lessons in expertise and efficiency, cultural xenophobia, corporate contempt, and advertising overkill).

As for the cultural exception that is France, contrary to what a recently dismissed CEO had to say, it is not dead: it consists in churning out exceptionally tedious movies, exceptionally slapdash books, and, all in all, works of art that are exceptionally pedantic and self-satisfied. It goes without saying that I include my own work in this sorry assessment.

8:35

THE LOBBY TO WINDOWS ON THE WORLD IS BEIGE. EVERYTHING important in America is magnolia. The walls are comforting, the carpet is thick, eggshell with a geometric pattern. Your loafers sink into the deep wool pile. The ground seems soft; that should have set us thinking.

"Keep quiet!"

Half past eight and already the kids are hyper. How old are we when we start to wake up exhausted? I can't stop yawning, while they're running around all over the place, zigzagging between the tables, almost knocking over an old lady with lilac hair.

"Stop it, guys!"

I try glaring at them, but still they don't behave. I have no control over my sons; even when I get angry, they think I'm just kidding. They're right: I am kidding. I don't really believe it. Like all parents of my generation, I'm incapable of being strict. Our kids are badly brought up because they're not brought up at all. At least, not by us; they're brought up by cartoon channels. Thank you, Disney Channel, the world's babysitter! Our kids are spoiled rotten, because we're spoiled rotten. Jerry and

David wind me up, but they have something over their mother; at least I still love them. That's why I'm letting them cut class this week. They're completely ecstatic about skipping school! I slump into my rust-colored chair and look around at the incredible view. "Unbelievable," the brochure said: for once the advertising doesn't lie. I'm blinded by the sunlight on the Atlantic. The skyscrapers carve out the blue like a cardboard stage set. In the United States, life is like a movie, since all movies are shot on location. All Americans are actors, and their houses, their cars, and their desires all seem artificial. Truth is reinvented every morning in America. It's a country that has decided to look like something on celluloid.

"Sir . . ."

The waitress is none too pleased at having to play cop. She brings back Jerry and David, who've just stolen a doughnut from a pair of stockbrokers and are using it as a Frisbee. I should slap them, but I can't help smiling. I get up to apologize to the doughnut's owners. They both work for Cantor Fitzgerald: a blonde who is sexy despite her Ralph Lauren suit (do girls really dress like that anymore?) and a stocky dark-haired man who seems cool in his Kenneth Cole suit. You don't need to be a P.I. to work out they're lovers. Would you take your wife to breakfast at the top of the World Trade Center? No . . . You leave your old lady at home and invite a colleague from the office for an early morning tryst (the yuppie version of an afternoon tryst). I eavesdrop, I love listening at keyholes, especially when there aren't any.

"I'm pretty bullish about the NASDAQ at the moment . . ." says the blonde in Ralph Lauren.

"Merrill's been upgrading the banking sector just on spec," says the guy in Kenneth Cole.

"Leave your wife," says the blonde in Ralph Lauren.

"So we can be a normal couple?" says the guy in Kenneth Cole.

"We'd never be a normal couple," says the blonde in Ralph Lauren.

"You don't hear me asking you to leave your husband," says the guy in Kenneth Cole.

"I would if you asked me to," says the blonde in Ralph Lauren.

"What we've got is special because it's impossible," says the guy in Kenneth Cole.

"I'm sick of only getting to see you in the morning or the afternoon," says the blonde in Ralph Lauren.

"I'm worse at night," says the guy in Kenneth Cole.

"Jeffrey Skilling invited me to L.A. in his private jet this weekend," says the blonde in Ralph Lauren.

"Yeah? And how are you going to get that one past your husband?" says the guy in Kenneth Cole.

"None of your business," says the blonde in Ralph Lauren.

"If you do that, you'll never see me again," says the guy in Kenneth Cole.

"You're jealous of Mike but you don't care about my husband?" says the blonde in Ralph Lauren.

"You haven't fucked your husband for two years," says the guy in Kenneth Cole.

"Leave your wife," says the blonde in Ralph Lauren.

"You really feel bullish about the NASDAQ?" says the guy in Kenneth Cole.

8:36

"THE WINDOWS OF THE WORLD" IS THE TITLE OF A SONG BY BURT Bacharach and Hal David recorded by Dionne Warwick in 1967. The lyrics? They were written in protest of the Vietnam war:

The windows of the world are covered with rain,
Where is the sunshine we once knew?
Ev'rybody knows when little children play
They need a sunny day to grow straight and tall.
Let the sun shine through.

The windows of the world are covered with rain,
When will those black skies turn to blue?
Ev'rybody knows when boys turn to men
They start to wonder when their country will call.
Let the sun shine through.

I wonder whether the owner of Windows on the World was familiar with the song.

8:37

THE KIDS ARE BORED NOW AND IT'S MY FAULT, BRINGING THEM TO places for oldsters. But they were the ones who insisted! I thought the view would keep them occupied, but that's done and dusted pretty quickly. They're like their dad: they get bored with everything pretty quickly. A generation of frantic channel-hopping and schizophrenic existentialism. What will they do when they find out they can't have everything, be everything? I feel sorry for them, because it's something I never got over myself.

I always feel weird when I see my kids. I'd like to be able to say "I love you," but it's too late. When they were three, I would tell them I loved them until they fell asleep. In the morning I'd wake them by tickling their feet. Their feet were always cold, always sticking out from under the duvet. But they're too macho now; they'd tell me to get lost. And I never look after them, don't get to see them enough; I'm not part of their routine anymore. Instead of saying "I love you," this is what I should say:

"There are worse things in life than having an absent father: having a present father. Some day you'll thank me for not smothering you. You'll realize I was helping you find your wings, pampering you from afar."

But this time, it's too soon. They will understand when they're my age: forty-three. It's strange, two brothers who are inseparable but always fighting. There's no need to pity us this morning. The Rice Krispies keep them occupied for a bit: Snap, Crackle, Pop. We talk about this stolen vacation when they should be back at school. David wants to go to Universal Studios again. He spent the whole year showing off in his I SURVIVED JURASSIC PARK T-shirt. He didn't even want to put it in the wash. Is there anything more arrogant than a seven-year-old? Later, kids learn self-discipline; there's less showing off. Take Jerry, for example, two years older and already he's a man, he has self-control, he knows how to compromise. He thinks he's all that, too, in his Eminem sweatshirt, but at least he makes less of a deal of it: he's the big brother. David's always sick with something, I hate hearing him coughing all the time; it winds me up, and I can't work out if it's the sound of the coughing that winds me up, or whether it's anxiety, some sort of paternal love. Deep down, what annoys me is never being sure that I'm good, but being absolutely certain that I'm selfish.

A Brazilian businessman lights a cigar. You have to be mad to smoke at this time of the morning. I beckon the maître d', who rushes over to him since; like almost every other restaurant in the city, Windows is non-smoking. The guy pretends this is the first he's heard of it, pretends to be shocked, demands to be shown the smoking section. The maître d' explains that he'll have to go down to the street! Rather than stub out his cigar, the smoker gets up and does just that, sprinting towards the elevator; no doubt a matter of honor.

8:38

. . . THEREBY PROVING THAT A CIGAR CAN SAVE YOUR LIFE. THEY should put a new health warning on cigarette packs: SMOKING CAN CAUSE YOU TO LEAVE BUILDINGS BEFORE THEY BLOW UP.

I would like to be able to change things, to scream at Carthew to get the fuck out of there, fast, GET OUT, TAKE THE KIDS AND MAKE A RUN FOR IT, TELL THE OTHERS, QUICK, GET A FUCKING MOVE ON, THE WHOLE PLACE IS GOING TO BLOW! GET THE FUCK OUT OF THE FUCKING BUILDING!!

Powerlessness, a writer's vanity. A useless book, like all books. The writer is like the cavalry, always arriving too late. The Maine-Montparnasse tower is wider on the rue du Départ side: if you wanted to fly a plane into it, you should aim for that side. I'm beginning to fall in love with this building that everyone loathes. I love it at night as much as I loathe it in daylight. Darkness is good for its complexion. In daylight, it is grayish, sad, hulking; only the night makes it brilliant, electric, with the little lights at each corner like a lighthouse in Paris. At night, the tower makes me think of the monolith in *2001: A Space Odyssey:* the tall, black rectangular slab, which is supposed to symbolize eternity. Last night, I took my fiancée to the night club in the basement of the tower. The club used to be called Inferno, but they've just renamed it Red Light. There was a twenty-fifth-anniversary party for *VSD* magazine: the place was heaving, lines for the coat check, sponsors, DJs, a couple of VIPs, nothing special. I hugged my darling to me and kissed her at the French equivalent of Ground Zero. I'd quite happily have had her in the restroom, but she refused:

"Sorry, tonight my pussy is observing Ramadan!"

I'd like to apologize to the Muslim authorities in advance for the preceding joke. I know perfectly well that it is permitted to eat at night during Ramadan. Be magnanimous. There's no need for a fatwa: I'm famous enough already. The year 2002 was a pretty complicated year for me. I had a great time and made a complete fool of myself. Let's not add to that in 2003, if you don't mind. Apparently the Tour Montparnasse is in no danger of an attack by Islamic fundamentalists, because it houses the French offices of Al Jazeera. I focus on this lightning rod as I dip my toast into my coffee.

The Tour Montparnasse is 656 feet high. To get an idea of the size of the World Trade Center, stack one Tour Montparnasse on top of another, and it would still be smaller than the World Trade Center. Every morning, the elevator takes 35 seconds to take me to Le Ciel de Paris (56th floor); I've timed it. In the elevator my feet feel heavy and my ears pop. This type of rapid elevator creates the same sensation as a plane in an air pocket—without the seatbelt. Le Ciel de Paris is all that remains of the Windows on the World: an idea. The preposterous and pretentious idea of a restaurant at the top of a tower that dominates the skyline. Here, the decor is black with a ceiling mimicking a starry sky. There aren't many people this morning because the weather is gloomy. People cancel their reservations when visibility is poor. Le Ciel de Paris is in a sea of fog. You can see nothing but white smoke from the windows. Pressing my nose up against the glass, I can make out the adjoining streets. When I was little, people often told me off for having my head in the clouds; nothing's changed. The Parker Knoll chairs probably date from the seventies; they'll be back in fashion soon. The black and tan carpet looks like something out of a no-budget indie movie. There is a continual background noise: the air conditioning purrs like a nuclear reactor. I press my face to the glass: a layer of mist shrouds the rue de Rennes. I'm sitting in a booth padded with brown leather like the ones in the Drugstore Publicis in Saint-Germain (a place that, like Windows on the World, has also disappeared). I've ordered freshly squeezed orange juice and some *viennoiseries* (three shriveled mini chocolate croissants). The waitress wears an orange uniform (she'll come back into fashion too). She brings me the croissants wrapped in a beige napkin. Maybe the Al Qaeda terrorists were simply sick to death of beige, orange uniforms, and the businesslike smile of the waitresses.

I feel like shit, sitting here all alone in Le Ciel de Paris at 8:38 A.M., a long way above the motorists honking their horns in front of the cinemas in Montparnasse, high above the employees of the Banque National de Paris, 656 feet more stratospheric than ordinary mortals. My life is a disaster, but nobody notices, because I'm too polite—I smile constantly. I smile because I think that if you hide your suffering, it disappears. And it's true, in a sense: it is invisible, and therefore it does not exist, since we live in a world that worships what is visible, demonstrable, material. My suffering is not material; it is hidden. I am my own revisionist.

8:39

As I finish my cappuccino, I look at the other customers, who do not look at me. A lot of sporty redheads. There's a table of Japanese tourists taking photos of each other. There's the adulterous stockbrokers. There are American tourists like me, nouveau riche rednecks and proud of it, WASPs wearing suspenders, yuppies with brilliant white teeth. Boys in striped shirts. Women with ultra–blow-dried hair, their pretty hands sporting long manicured nails. Most of them look like Britney Spears will twenty years from now. There are Arabs, Englishmen, Pakistanis, Brazilians, Italians, Vietnamese, Mexicans, all of them fat. What the customers of Windows on the World have in common is their paunches. I wonder whether I wouldn't have been better off taking the kids to the Rainbow Room, on the 65th floor of the NBC building. The Rainbow Room: twenty-four windows in the heart of the city. The architects of Rockefeller Center wanted to call it the Stratosphere. But my kids wouldn't have appreciated the thirties mirrors, the reflections of Manhattan, the legacy of jazz big bands, the whiff of the Roaring Twenties. All Jerry and David want is to stuff themselves with sausage and muffins in the highest restaurant in New York. Luckily for my wallet, the Toys R Us in the lobby was closed, otherwise they'd have cleaned the place out. My kids are tyrants, and I have to follow their orders to the letter. As I bolt my breakfast, I look down: from this height it's impossible to make out people. The only moving things in Lower Manhattan are the cars coming and going across the Brooklyn Bridge, tourist helicopters over the East River, and the boats passing each other under the suspension bridges. I'd copied a quote from Kafka into the guidebook: "The bridge connecting New York with Brooklyn hung delicately over the East River, and if one half-shut one's eyes it seemed to tremble. It appeared to be quite bare of traffic, and beneath it stretched a smooth empty tongue of water." Amazing how he can so accurately describe something he never saw. Directly in front of me, I can see the Chase Manhattan Building, to the left the Manhattan Bridge, and to the right, at the end of Fulton Street, South Street Seaport, but I would be incapable of describing them. And I realize that I love this crazy country of mine, the fucked-up times we live in, my annoying kids. A surge of affection overwhelms me—probably last night's vodka catching up with me. Candace took me to Pravda, and we kind of overdid it on the cherry vodka. Candace did a photo shoot for Victoria's Secret—I mention it just to give you an idea of how hot she is. But things aren't going too well between us: she wants us to get married, have a baby, live together, and these are precisely the three mistakes that I want to avoid making again. To punish me for wanting to stay single, she doesn't come anymore when we fuck. They say some women say no when they mean yes; Candace is the opposite: when she says yes, she means no.

* * *

"Why are you so bullish about the NASDAQ?" asks the guy in Kenneth Cole.

"You can't lose now that the Internet bubble's burst," says the blonde in Ralph Lauren. "Pretty much anything's gonna run up three sticks. The stocks have completely crunched."

"Yeah, but look at the cash flows—it's all off-balance-sheet transactions," says the guy in Kenneth Cole, "I'd be worried about getting jigged out."

"I bought some stock in Enron," says the blonde in Ralph Lauren. "The company's a scalper's dream. Have you seen their earnings?"

"I'm with you there, almost worth holding a position on. WorldCom, too. Their EBITDA is sweet as a million-dollar bill," says the guy in Kenneth Cole. "Otherwise I don't fancy being a bottom fisher in that market."

"Yeah, well, one way or the other, 2001 is gonna be shit. All the bonuses are going to be slashed," says the blonde in Ralph Lauren. "You can kiss your villa in Hawaii goodbye."

"I think it's pretty simple: fuck the Porsche, I'm holding liquid," says the guy in Kenneth Cole. "But 2002 has got to be better. We just have to wait and see what Greenspan does on rates."

"I love you," says the blonde in Ralph Lauren.

"God, I want to launch a hostile takeover bid on you," says the guy in Kenneth Cole.

"Leave your fucking wife," says the blonde in Ralph Lauren.

"OK, OK, I promise I'll dump her tonight, soon as I get in from the gym," says the guy in Kenneth Cole.

And they launch into a pretty hot kiss, all tongues and spit like a good California porn movie or a perfume ad.

8:40

THE GUIDEBOOKS ALL GAVE WINDOWS ON THE WORLD GLOWING reviews. Here at the top of the Tour Montparnasse on a September morning in 2002, I leaf through them. A year after the tragedy, they take on a strange resonance. For example, the *Michelin Green Guide 2000* writes:

"**Windows on the World**, One World Trade Center (107th floor). This elegant restaurant bar boasts the most stunning panoramic views of New York. Since the infamous bombing attempt in 1993, considerable renovation has allowed it to reinvent itself with a sumptuous new interior."

The World Trade Center was a target; something even the guidebooks realized. It was no secret. On February 26, 1993, at 12:18 P.M., a bomb in a van in the parking lot exploded. The basement of the World Trade Center collapsed. A deep crater, six dead and a thousand injured. The towers were refurbished and reopened within a month.

Frommer's Guide 2000 is more effusive:

"**Windows on the World** (West St. between Liberty and Vesey). Main $25–35; sunset menu (before 6 P.M.) $35; brunch

$32.50. Cards: VISA. Subway: C, E, World Trade Center. Valet parking on West Street, $18. The interiors are sober but pleasing. In any case, they are of little importance as, just outside the 'Windows' all of New York is unfurled! The restaurant offers unassailable views of the city. And with Michael Lomonaco, former chef at the '21' Club, now at the helm, the Modern American cuisine is second to none. The cellar, too, is full to bursting. The sommelier is happy to point you in the right direction, whether you are a connoisseur or simply an amateur looking to ideally complement your char-grilled cutlets or Homard de Maine, two of Lomonaco's specialties."

In a magazine article, I read that two inseparable brothers worked side by side cleaning shellfish in the kitchens. Two Muslims.

What we know now leads us to look for portents everywhere; it's a foolish exercise that gives some restaurant review written in 2000 a prophetic significance. If we pick apart the previous review word by word, the text reads like something out of Nostradamus. "Just outside the 'Windows'"? An oncoming plane. "Unassailable views"? On the contrary, they were all too assailable. "The cellar, too, filled to bursting"? Absolutely: it will soon have 600,000 tons of rubble piled on top of it. "The sommelier is happy to point you in the right direction." Like an air-traffic controller. "Char-grilled cutlets"? Soon to be charred at 1,500 degrees. "Homard de Maine"—you mean Omar the Mullah? I know, it's not funny, you don't joke about death. I'm sorry, it's a form of self-defense: I write these jokes at the top of a tower in Paris, flicking through pages and pages of reviews for a sister site that no longer exists. It's impossible not to see portents everywhere, coded messages from the past. The past is now the only place where you can find Windows on the World.

This unique restaurant where you could enjoy a haute cuisine at the top of the world; where you had to reserve a table to take your mistress to admire the view so that you could leer into her low-cut blouse as she leaned down to check she had condoms in her handbag, this place magnificent, unique, unscathed, this place is called the past.

The *Hachette Guide 2000* commented, without realizing the cruel irony that the remark would one day have:

"The restaurant operates as a sort of private club at lunchtime, but for a small consideration, will admit you even if you are not a member."

Sic.

The paradox of the Twin Towers is that it was an ultramodern complex in the oldest neighborhood in New York, at the southernmost tip of Manhattan island: New Amsterdam. Now, the New York landscape has once more become as it was when Holden Caulfield ran away. The destruction of the Twin Towers takes the city back to 1965, the year in which I was born. It's strange to realize that I am exactly as old as the World Trade Center. This is the Manhattan in which Salinger wrote *The Catcher in the Rye* (1951), an American *Le grand Meaulnes*, which takes place in 1949. Do you know where the title of *The Catcher in the Rye* comes from?

It comes from a Robert Burns poem: "If a body meet a body coming through the rye." Holden Caulfield (the narrator) mishears the poem: he believes it runs "If a body catch a body coming through the rye." He decides he is "the catcher in the rye." This is what he would most like to do in life. On page 173, he explains his vocation to his little sister, Phoebe. He imagines himself running through the fields of rye trying to save thousands of kids. This would be his ideal profession. Darting around the field of rye, catching all the children running along the cliff top, clusters of innocent hearts tumbling into the void. Their carefree laughter whipped away on the breeze. Running through the rye in the sunshine. "Ev'rybody knows when little children play / They need a sunny day to grow straight and tall" ("The Windows of the World"). The most perfect of all possible destinies: catching them before they fall. I too would like to be the catcher.

The Catcher in the Windows.

8:41

I PRETEND TO SNEER AT THE PEOPLE AT THE NEARBY TABLES. IT'S ONE of my favorite games when the kids are getting on my nerves. Look at this bunch of nonentities: they're forgetting they're descended from Dutch, Irish, German, Italian, French, English, and Spanish settlers who came across the Atlantic three or four centuries ago. Well yee ha! I hit the big time! I've got a house on Long Island, two rosy-cheeked kids who say "shoot" instead of "shit"! I'm not some hick off the boat anymore. Soft expensive sheets, soft expensive TP, soft expensive flower-print curtains, and enough domestic appliances to make my wife with her lacquered hair drool. The American dream: *American Beauty*. Sometimes I think the movie's hero, Lester Burnham, is me. The cynical, phlegmatic guy bored shitless with his perfect family is "so me" a couple of years ago. Carthew Yorston walked out on his life from one day to the next. Actually I arranged to have myself kicked out of my own house: I'm not sure if it was cowardice or respect for Mary. In the film, his wife wants to kill him but in the end he's murdered by his homophobic ex-army neighbor. Let's just say that for the moment, at least, I'm doing better than Lester. But, Jesus, I jerked off so much in the shower. And then there's that brilliant phrase in the voiceover: "In a year, I'll be dead, but in a way, I am dead already." We have a lot in common, Lester Burnham and I.

Before long, I hope, my sons will be introducing me to their girlfriends. Uh-oh, I'm not too sure I'll be able to resist hitting on them like some dirty old man. I wonder what Jerry and David Yorston will do when they grow up. Will they be successful artists, rock stars, Hollywood actors, TV presenters? Maybe industrialists, bankers, ruthless businessmen? As a father, I hope they choose the second option, but as an American, I can't help but fantasize about the first. And in reality, they're most likely to end up realtors like their father. Forty years from now, when I'm incontinent and bedridden in Fort Lauderdale, they'll be changing my diapers. I'll eat dry crackers and fritter away their inheritance in some Florida gulag! It'll be great: I'll have my groceries delivered, order food online, and some hooker who looks like Farrah Fawcett in *Charlie's Angels* will suck my cock and smile. I love this country. Oh, yes, I forgot: I'll play golf, if I can still walk. Jerry and David will caddy for me.

Looking down through the telescope I can see a white cube: the piazza where minuscule restaurant employees are putting chairs out on the terraces for people to lunch in the midday sunshine. I assume ice-cream sellers are putting out their blackboards, and hotdog and pretzel vendors are setting up their carts round the WTC Plaza. That tiny cube? A stage for open-air rock concerts. That metal ball? A bronze globe sculpted by Fritz Koenig. There's a bunch of hideous contemporary sculptures: mountains of tangled, stacked, warped metal girders. I have no idea what the artists were trying to say.

It's Indian summer; I hum *Autumn in New York.*

Autumn in New York
Why does it seem so invitiiing?
Glittering crowwwds and shimmering clouuuds
In canyons of steeeel . . .
Autuuuum in Neeeew Yorrk
Is often mingled wiiith pain . . .
Dreaaamers with empty haaands
All sigh for exoootic lands . . .

Oscar Peterson on piano; Louis Armstrong on trumpet; vocal by Ella Fitzgerald.

I really must set up an appointment to have a vasectomy. In the beginning, with Candace, everything was perfect. I met her on the Internet (on www.match.com). These days Internet dates are a dime a dozen. Match.com has 8 million members worldwide. If you're visiting a foreign city, you set up a couple of dates before you arrive; it's as easy as booking a hotel room. After dinner on our first date, I invited her up to my room for a drink so we could chat some more, and normally, that's where she should have turned me down, because that's the rule: never fuck on a first date. You know what she did? She looked me right in the eye and said: "If I'm coming up, it won't be to chat." Wow. Together, we went too far too fast: X-rated pay-per-view movies, mutual masturbation and ass fucking using dildos and vibrators; we even went to a swingers' club, but she wound me up—she had the best orgasm of her life with some ham-fisted kid with earrings and a skinhead! How do you know a Texan at an orgy? He's the only one having a jealous fit. Ever since, the sex has been good, but a bit healthier. Like a merger between two lonely egomaniacs, we use each other's bodies to get off, and sometimes I think both of us are forcing ourselves. Hmm. She's probably cheating on me; couples cheat on each other earlier and earlier these days.

8:42

I'VE GOT A PROBLEM: I DON'T REMEMBER MY CHILDHOOD.

The only thing I remember is that being middle class doesn't buy happiness.

Darkness; everything is dark. My alarm clock goes off, it's eight o'clock, I'm late, I'm thirteen years old, I slip on my brown Kickers, drag my huge army surplus bag full of Stypens, correction pens, textbooks as heavy as they are fucking boring. Mom is already up heating some milk, my brother and I slurp it noisily, bitching because there's skin on the milk, before taking the elevator down into this dark winter morning in 1978. The Lycée Louis-le-Grand is miles away. It's on the rue Coëtlogon, 75006 Paris. I'm dying of cold and boredom. I stuff my hands in my ugly loden coat. I huddle myself up in my itchy yellow scarf. I know it's going to rain and I've missed the 84. What I don't know is that this whole thing is absurd, that none of this will ever come in useful. Neither do I know that this dismal dawn is the only morning in my whole childhood that I will later remember. I don't even know why I'm sad—maybe because I haven't got the balls to cut math class. Charles decides to wait for the bus, and I decide to walk to school, past the Jardin de Luxembourg, along the rue de Vaugirard, where Scott and Zelda Fitzgerald lived from April to August 1928 (at the corner of the rue Bonaparte), but I didn't know that then. I still live nearby; from my balcony I can see kids with the schoolbags rushing to school, spewing plumes of cold breath: tiny hunchbacked dragons running along the sidewalk, avoiding the cracks. They watch their feet, careful not to step on the gaps between the paving stones as if they're walking through a minefield. Bleak is the adjective that best sums up my life back then. *Bleak* as an icy morning. At that moment, I'm convinced nothing interesting will ever happen to me. I'm ugly, skinny, I feel completely alone, and the sky buckets down on me. I stand, soaked to the skin, in front of the Senate, which is gray as my shitty school: everything about school pisses me off: the walls, the teachers, the pupils. I hold my breath; things are awful, everything's awful, why is everything so awful? Because I'm ordinary, because I'm thirteen, because I've got a chin like a gumboot, because I'm scrawny. If I'm going to be this scrawny I might as well be dead. A bus comes and I hesitate, I really hesitate, I almost threw myself under the bus that day. It's the 84 overtaking me with Charles inside. The big wheels splatter the bottoms of my stupid pleated pants (beige corduroy with cuffs that are way too big). I walk toward normality. I walk, wheezing, across the black ice. No girl will ever love me, and I can see their point, I don't hold it against you, *mesdemoiselles*, I can see your point: even I don't love me. I'm late: Madame Minois, my math teacher, will roll her eyes to heaven and spit. The cretins in my class will heave a sigh just to make themselves look good. Rain will stream down the windowpanes of a classroom that reeks of despair (despair, I now know, smells of chalk dust).

Why am I complaining when there's nothing wrong with me? I haven't been raped, beaten, abandoned, drugged. Just divorced parents who are excessively kind to me, like every kid in my class. I'm traumatized by my lack of trauma. That morning, I choose to live. I walk through the school gates like walking into a lion's den. The building has a black mouth, its windows are yellow eyes. It swallows me in order to feed on me. I'm completely submissive. I agree to become what they make of me. I come face to face with my adolescent spinelessness.

From the top of the Tour Montparnasse I can, if I try, make out the School of my Wasted Youth. I still live in this neighborhood where I suffered so much. I do not leave this place that made me who I am. I never rebelled. I never even moved house. From my house, to get to my job at Flammarion, I walk down the same rue de Vaugirard as the little boy whose ears and hands were frozen. I spew the same plumes of cold breath. I still do not walk on the cracks. I never escaped that morning.

8:43

MY CHILDHOOD TAKES PLACE IN THE VERDANT PARADISE OF A FASHIONABLE suburb of Austin, Texas. A house that looks just like the neighbors', a garden where we drink from the fountain, an open-top Chevy driving toward the desert. Through the window, a sofa and a TV reflected in the faces of two children, and at this time of the day it's the same all over town, all over the country. My parents try their best to live like a Technicolor movie: they hold cocktail parties at which the mothers compare notes on interior decoration. Every year, we consume an average of four tons of crude oil. High school? Nothing but pimply white kids in baseball caps listening to the Grateful Dead and squashing beer cans against their foreheads. Nothing too serious. Sunshine, coffee shops, football tryouts, cheerleaders with big tits who say "I mean" and "like" in every sentence. Everything about my adolescence is clean: lap-dancing bars don't exist yet, and motels are R-rated. I eat lunch on the grass, play tennis, read comics in the hammock. Ice cubes go "clink clink" in my father's glass of scotch. There are a couple of executions every week in my state. My childhood unfolds on a lawn. Don't get me wrong: we're not talking *Little House on the Prairie*, more Little Bungalow in the Suburbs. I wear braces on my teeth, take my wooden Dunlop tennis racket and play air guitar in front of the mirror with the radio full blast. I spend my vacations at summer camp, I go river rafting in dinghies, hone my serve, win at water polo, discover masturbation thanks to *Hustler*. All the Lolitas are in love with Cat Stevens, but since he's not around they lose their cherries to the tennis coach. My greatest trauma is the film *King Kong* (the 1933 version): my folks had gone out and my sister and I secretly watched it in their bedroom despite our babysitter's injunction. The black and white image of this enormous gorilla scaling the Empire State Building, snatching the army planes out of the sky, is my worst childhood memory. They did a remake in color in the seventies which uses the World Trade Center. Any minute now I expect to see a huge gorilla scaling the towers—believe it or not I've got goose bumps right now, I can't stop thinking about it.

You can thumb through my life in high school yearbooks. I thought it was happy at the time, but thinking back on it, it depresses me. Maybe because I'm scared that it's over, scared because I've left my old family to make a killing in real estate. I became successful at it the day I realized a very simple thing: you don't make money on big properties, you make it on little ones (because you sell more of them). Middle-class families read the same magazines as rich ones: everyone wants that apartment in *Wallpaper*, or a loft just like Lenny Kravitz's! So I did a deal with a credit union, who agreed to lend me a couple of million dollars over thirty years, then I found a bunch of old cattle warehouses in an old cowboy section of Austin and transformed them into artists' studios for idiots. My genius was my ability to convince couples who came to me that their loft was unique when in fact I was shifting thirty a year. That's how I climbed the greasy pole at the agency, stole the job of the guy who hired me, then set up my own company, Austin Maxi Real Estate. Three point five million, soon be four. Hardly Donald Trump, but it's enough to take the long view. Like my dad used to say: "The first million is the hardest, after that the rest just follow!" Jerry and David are financially comfortable, though they don't realize that yet, because I always play the part of an aristocrat on his uppers in front of Mary so she doesn't force me to quadruple the alimony. Strangely, money is the reason I left her: I couldn't keep going home when I had all that dough burning a hole in my pocket. What was the point of earning all that money if I was going to be stuck with the same woman every night? I wanted to be the antithesis of George Babbitt, that dumb schmuck incapable of escaping his family and his town. . . .

"Gimme the camera," says David.

"No, it's mine," says Jerry.

"You don't know how to take photos," says David.

"You don't either," says Jerry.

"You didn't even set the flash," says David.

"You don't have to when it's bright," says Jerry.

"An' you didn't set the speed," says David.

"Who cares? It's only a disposable," says Jerry.

"Take one of the Statue of Liberty," says David.

"Already took one," says Jerry.

"Last time they were all blurry," says David.

"Shut up," says Jerry.

"Gimp," says David.

"Gimp yourself," says Jerry.

"Jerry's a gimp, Jerry's a gimp, Jerry's a gimp," says David.

"Takes one to know one," says Jerry.

"C'mon," David says. "Gimme the camera."

8:44

IF THEY COULD STUDY THE PHOTOS THEY'RE TAKING CAREFULLY (photos that will never be developed), behind the Empire State Building, Jerry and David would notice a white dot moving on the horizon. Like a dazzling white gull against the blue skyline. But birds don't fly this high, nor this fast. Sunlight ricochets off the silver shape like when one of the guys in *Mission: Impossible* flashes a mirror in his partner's eyes to signal to him without making any noise.

In Le Ciel de Paris, everything is designed to constantly remind you that you are higher that the normal. Even in the restrooms, the walls with the urinals show the skyline of the City of Light, so that male customers can piss all over it.

I should come back and have dinner here: the menu is pretty tempting. "Autumn in Le Ciel de Paris as interpreted by Jean-François Oyon and his team": among the appetizers is seared foie gras on *pain d'épices* with a cream of *ceps* (€25.50); fish dishes include fillet of gray mullet *a la plancha* with a bouillabaisse reduction and eggplant remoulade (€26.00); if you prefer meat,

Jean-François Oyon suggests pigeon roasted in honey and spices with caramelized cabbage (€33.00). For dessert I'd be tempted to go for the luxurious warm, chocolate "Guanaja" with hazelnut cream ice. I realize it's hardly good for your health—Karl Lagerfeld would disapprove—but I prefer something luxurious to the Tonka and morello cherry surprise or even the roasted figs with Bourbon vanilla butter.

Behind me, a terrible drama is unfolding: an American couple are demanding ham and eggs with mushrooms for their breakfast, but the waitress in her orange uniform says "I'm sorry, *nous ne servons que du* continental breakfast." A repast composed of toast, croissants or *pains au chocolat*, fruit juice and coffee, the continental breakfast is rather less substantial than the breakfast Americans are accustomed to ingesting in the morning. Accordingly they stand up, cursing loudly, and walk out of the restaurant. They can't understand how such a touristy place can be incapable of serving a decent, ample breakfast. From a strictly commercial viewpoint, they're not wrong. But what's the point in traveling if it's to eat the same things you eat at home? In fact, it's a terrible misunderstanding—everyone is right. Le Ciel de Paris should give its customers a choice, offer as wide a selection at breakfast as they do at dinner. And Americans should stop trying to export their lifestyle to the entire planet. That said, that's two people who would survive if an airplane did crash into the Tour Montparnasse at 8:46 this morning, as it did into the North Tower of the World Trade Center on September 11, 2001.

What is staggering is that a plane had already flown into a New York skyscraper. On a foggy night in 1945, an American B-25 bomber crashed into the Empire State Building between floors 78 and 79. Fourteen dead and a colossal inferno several hundred feet high. But the Empire State did not collapse because the building's steel structure did not buckle as the World Trade Center did (steel loses its rigidity at 840°F and melts at 2,500°F, whereas the heat given off by the two Boeings is estimated to have been 3,600°F). In 2001, the 10,500 gallons of flaming jet fuel destroyed the metallic structure of the buildings, and the upper floors collapsed onto those beneath. In order to build the Twin Towers, architect Minoru Yamasaki had used a new technique: instead of using a maze of internal columns, he chose to rest the greater part of the weight on the external walls, which were composed of tightly-spaced vertical steel pillars connected by horizontal girders that girdled the towers at each floor. This architecture allowed him to maximize the interior space (and thereby earn more money for the property developers). It was these pillars, covered with a thin coating of aluminum, which gave the two towers the banded appearance of two hi-fi speakers.

Conclusion: the Twin Towers were built to withstand the impact of a plane *without fuel*.

Welcome to the minute before. The point at which everything is still possible. They could decide to leave on the spur of the moment. But Carthew thinks they still have time, they should make the most of their New York jaunt; the kids seem happy. Customers are leaving: at any moment, customers enter and leave the restaurant. Look, the old lady Jerry and David were pestering earlier—the one with the lilac hair—is getting up; she's already paid the check (not forgetting to leave a five-dollar tip); slowly she makes her way to the elevator. The two badly behaved children have reminded her that she needs to buy a present for her grandson's birthday; she says "Have a nice day" to the receptionist and presses the button marked MEZZANINE, the button lights up, a bell goes "ding"; she decides she'll stroll around the mall for a little. She thinks she remembers seeing a branch of Toys R Us but can't remember whether it was in the basement or the mezzanine. This is what she is thinking as the doors to the elevator close noiselessly. For the rest of her life, she will believe it was the Lord God who told her to leave at this precise moment; for the rest of her life she will wonder why He did so, why He spared her life, why He made her think of toys, why He chose her and not the two little boys.

8:45

A MINUTE BEFORE, THE STATE OF AFFAIRS WAS RECOVERABLE. THEN suddenly I got the jitters.

"Hey, what's the difference between David Lynch and Merrill Lynch?" asks the guy in Kenneth Cole.

"Um . . . No, don't know that one," says the blonde in Ralph Lauren.

"There isn't one: nobody has a clue what either of them are doing and both of them are losing money," says the guy in Kenneth Cole.

They burst out laughing, then think better of it and revert to their professionalism.

"It's more volatile but the volumes are down," says the blonde in Ralph Lauren.

"Standard and Poor's futures are scary," says the guy in Kenneth Cole.

"The margins are killing us all," says the blonde in Ralph Lauren.

"I'm going long on the NASDAQ," says the guy in Kenneth Cole.

"The squiggly lines aren't looking good," says the blonde in Ralph Lauren.

"Sometimes you gotta know when to cut your arm off," says the guy in Kenneth Cole.

"We got whacked on the yen," says the blonde in Ralph Lauren.

"Well, my position on the Nikkei is covered," says the guy in Kenneth Cole.

"Oh my God," says the blonde in Ralph Lauren, "OH MY GOD!"

Her eyes grow wide, her bottom lip has fallen as far from her upper lip as it can, she's brought her trembling hand up to her frozen mouth.

"What? What is it? WHAT'S THE PROBLEM?" demands the guy in Kenneth Cole, before turning around.

The weather had been so beautiful: through the telescope, Jerry could count the rivets on the fuselage. He turned to me, all excited:

"Look, Dad! See the plane?"

—but already my hands had betrayed me. In a split second I'd contracted Parkinson's. Other customers realized what was happening: an American Airlines jet, a fucking Boeing, was flying low through New York, heading straight for us.

"Shit! What the fuck is he doing? He's far too low!"

I hate disaster movies: the good-natured blond guy with the square jaw, the pregnant woman whose waters break, the paranoid guy who freaks out, the coward who turns out to be a hero, the priest giving the last rites. There's always some idiot who gets sick, and the stewardess goes looking for a doctor:

"Is there a doctor on the plane?"

And some medical student puts his hand up; he feels really useful. "Don't sweat it, guys, everything's gonna be fine."

This is what you think when there's a Boeing heading straight for you. What a pain in the ass, starring in a turkey like that. You don't think anything, you hang on to the armrests. You don't believe your eyes. You hope what's happening isn't happening. You hope your body is lying to you. For once, you hope your senses are wrong, that your eyes are deceiving you. I'd like to tell you my first thought was for Jerry and David, but it wasn't. I didn't instinctively try to protect them. When I dived under the table, I wasn't thinking of anyone except little old me.

8:46

We now know with reasonable certainty what happened at 8:46 a.m. An American Airlines Boeing 767 with 92 people on board, 11 of them crew, flew into the north face of One World Trade Center, between floors 94 and 98; 10,500 gallons of jet fuel immediately burst into flames in the offices of Marsh & McLennan. It was flight AA11 (Boston–Los Angeles), which had taken off from Logan Airport at 7:59 a.m. and was moving at 500 mph. The force of such an impact is estimated as being equivalent to an explosion of 265 tons of dynamite (a 12-second shock wave measuring 0.9 on the Richter scale). We also know that none of the 1,344 people trapped on the 19 floors above survived. Obviously, this piece of information removes any element of suspense from this book. So much the better: this isn't a thriller; it is simply an attempt—doomed, perhaps—to describe the indescribable.

Genesis 11:1–3

"And the whole earth was of one language, and of one speed. And it came to pass, as they journeyed from the east, that they found a plain in the land of Shinar; and they dwelt there. And they said to one another, Go to, let us make brick, and burn them thoroughly. And they had brick for stone, and slime they had for mortar."

8:47

When an American Airlines Boeing 767 slams into a building below your feet, there are two immediate consequences. First, the skyscraper becomes a metronome, and I can assure you that when One World Trade Center starts to think it's the Leaning Tower of Pisa, it feels pretty strange. This is what experts refer to as the shock wave; it makes you feel like you're in a boat in a roaring storm or, to use a metaphor my kids would understand, like being inside a giant blender for three or four seconds. Glasses of juice shatter on the floor, lights come away from the walls and dangle from wires; wooden ceilings collapse, and the sound of breaking crockery comes from the kitchens. In the bar, bottles roll and explode. Bouquets of sunflowers topple, and vases shatter into a thousand pieces. Champagne buckets spill onto the carpet. Dessert trolleys skate down the aisles. Faces tremble as much as the walls.

Second, your ears burn as the fireball passes the window, then everything is swathed in thick smoke; it seeps from the floor, the walls, the elevator shafts, the air vents; tracking down an incredible number of openings designed to let in fresh air and now doing the reverse: the ventilation system becomes a fumigation system. Immediately, people start to cough and cover their mouths with napkins. This time, I remember the existence of Jerry and David: all three of us were huddled under the table. I doused napkins in the jug of orange juice before giving one to each of them.

"Breathe through the cloth. It's a test: they do this kind of thing in New York—they call it a fire drill. There's nothing to worry about, darlings, actually it's pretty fun, isn't it?"

"Dad, did the plane crash into the tower Dad, WHASHAPP-NINGDAAD?"

"No, of course not." I smile. "Don't worry, boys, it's all special effects, but I wanted it to be a surprise: it's a new attraction, the plane was a 3D movie—George Lucas did the special effects, they do a false alert here every morning. Really scared you though, huh?"

"But, Dad, the whole place is shaking, and the waitresses are scared and they're screaming . . ."

"Don't worry, they use hydraulics to make the restaurant shake, like they do in theme parks. And the waitresses are actors, they're just plants put in among the paying customers, like in Pirates of the Caribbean! Remember Pirates of the Caribbean, Dave?"

"Sure, Dad. So what's this ride called?"

"Tower Inferno."

"Right . . . Fuck, sure feels real . . ."

"Dave, we don't say 'fuck,' even in a towering inferno, OK?"

Jerry seemed less reassured than David by my Benigni-style play-acting, but since it was the first thing I could think of, I decided I have to run with it, so that he wouldn't immediately start crying. If Jerry started crying, I couldn't be sure that I wouldn't cry too, and then David was likely to get in on the act. But David never cries, and he certainly wasn't going to start now.

"You have to admit the special effects are pretty mind-blowing: the smoke coming out of everywhere, and all the customers who're paid to panic, it's pretty well put together!"

Around us, people were getting to their feet, still staring at each other, petrified. Some who'd dived under the table like we did looked up now, a little embarrassed that they weren't hero material. Jerry's pancakes were lying on the floor, covered with bits of porcelain. The pot of maple syrup dripped between the overturned chairs. Outside the Windows on the World, you couldn't see a thing: a dense black curtain blocked the view. Night had fallen, New York had disappeared, and the ground rumbled. I can tell you, everyone in the place had only one idea, neatly summed up by the head chef:

"We've got to get the hell out of here."

Now that I think about it, I *would* like to have been in one of those brainless disaster movie blockbusters. Because pretty much all of them have a happy ending.

8:48

OTHER POSSIBLE NAMES FOR THE WORLD TRADE CENTER RESTAU-rant:

- Windows on the Planes
- Windows on the Crash
- Windows on the Smoke
- Broken Windows

Sorry for that bout of black humor: a momentary defense against the atrocity.

The *New York Times* collated a number of eyewitness accounts of Windows on the World at that moment. Two amateur videos show smoke seeping into the upper floors at incredible speed. Paradoxically, the restaurant is more smoky than the floors just above the point of impact, because the smoke has taken some fifty feet to thicken. We have fragments of a call made by Rajesh Mirpuri to his boss, Peter Lee at Data Synapse. He says he can't see more than ten feet. The situation is rapidly deteriorating. At

Cantor Fitzgerald (on the 104th floor), fire blocks the elevators. Employees take refuge in the offices on the north face, fifty of them in a single conference room.

At that moment, the majority still believe this is an accident. There is considerable evidence to suggest that most of them were still alive until the building collapsed at 10:28 A.M. They suffered for 102 minutes, the average running time of a Hollywood film.

Extract from *Against the Grain* by Joris-Karl Huysmans:

> It was the vast, foul bagnio of America transported to our Continent; it was, in a word, the limitless, unfathomable, incommensurable firmament of blackguardism of the financier and the self-made man, beaming down, like a despicable sun, on the idolatrous city that grovelled on its belly, hymning vile songs of praise before the impious tabernacle of Commerce.
>
> "Well, crumble then, society! perish, old world!" cried Des Esseintes, indignant at the ignominy of the spectacle he had conjured up . . .

I knew it. The person really responsible for this attack wasn't Osama bin Laden, but the incorrigible Des Esseintes. I thought that decadent dandy was behaving a little oddly. Having for so long found nihilism cool, spoiled children now root for serial killers. All those weird little boys who sniggeringly advocate hatred now have blood on their shirt fronts. No dry cleaner will ever get the blood spatters out of their designer vests. Dandyism is inhuman; the eccentrics, too cowardly to act, prefer to kill others rather than themselves. They murder the ill-dressed. Des Esseintes, with his pale hands, murders children whose only crime is to be ordinary. His snobbish contempt is a flamethrower.

How can anyone forgive the murder of the old woman in Florida on page 201 of my previous novel? We point the finger at those who are indirectly guilty, anonymous, impersonal pension funds, dummy organizations. But at the end of the day, those who scream, who plead, who bleed, are real. At the end of the world satire becomes reality, metaphor becomes truth, when even political cartoonists feel embarrassed. . . .

8:49

YOUR IMMEDIATE REACTION IS TO GRAB YOUR CELL PHONE. BUT since it's a first reflex, everyone else has had the same idea, and the networks are jammed. As I anxiously press the green REDIAL button, I try to convince the boys that this suffocating darkness is just a funfair ride.

"You'll see: any minute now they'll send in a fake rescue team. It's gonna be wicked! That black cloud is really well done, isn't it?"

The stockbroker couple look at me pityingly.

"Jesus," says the blonde in Ralph Lauren. "Let's get the hell out of this steam bath."

The dark-haired guy gets up and runs for the elevators, dragging his lover by the hand. I fall in behind, a child on each arm. But the elevators are out of order. Behind her desk, the receptionist is sobbing:

"I'm not trained for this kind of situation. . . . We're supposed to evacuate via the stairs. Follow me. . . ."

The majority of Windows on the World customers haven't waited for her. They're already crammed into the smoke-filled stairwell. They cough in single file. A black security guard throws up in a trash can. He's already been down four floors.

"I've just been down there, it's hell, don't go, the whole place is blazing!"

We go anyway. It's utter chaos: the crash has knocked out all means of communication with the outside world. I turn to Jerry and David, who have started whimpering.

"C'mon, kids, if we're gonna win the game, we can't let them think they've fooled us. So, no panicking, please, otherwise we'll be eliminated. Just follow your dad and we'll try and get downstairs. You both played Dungeons and Dragons, right? The winners are always the ones who are best at bluffing the enemy. If we show any signs of weakness, we'll lose the game, got it?"

The two brothers nod politely.

I realize I've forgotten to describe myself. I used to be striking; later I was handsome; later still, not so bad; now I'm alright. I read a lot of books, and underline the sentences I like (like all autodidacts) (that's why autodidacts are often the most cultivated people: they spend their whole life preparing for an exam they never took). On a good day I look like Bill Pullman, the actor (he was the President in *Independence Day*). On a bad day I look more like Robin Williams if he was prepared to play a Texan realtor with a funny walk, a receding hairline, and crow's-feet around the eyes (too much sun, yeah!). In a couple of years time, I'll be a perfectly good candidate for the George W. Bush lookalike contest; if I survive, that is.

Jerry's my oldest son; that's why he's so serious. The firstborn have to put up with the teething problems. He reminds me of my mother. I like the way he takes everything so seriously. I can get him to believe anything, he'll swallow anything, but afterward, he hates me for lying to him. Honest, sincere, brave: Jerry is the man I should have been. Sometimes I think he hates me. I think I disappoint him. Oh, well: it's a father's destiny to disappoint his son. Look at Luke Skywalker—his father is Darth Vader! Jerry is exactly like I was at his age: he believes in the order of things, he's impatient for everything to come good. Later, he'll lose his illusions. I hope he doesn't. I hope his eyes will always be so honest, so blue. I need you, Jerry. In the old days, kids depended on their parents to guide them. Now it's the opposite.

David, well, of course, being two years younger, David constantly doubts everything: his blond bangs, the point of going to school, the existence of Santa Claus or the Hanson brothers. He hardly ever talks, except to yank his brother's chain. In the beginning, Mary and I thought there might be something wrong with him: he's never cried in his life, even when he was born. He doesn't ask for anything, doesn't say anything, remains eloquently silent; but I know that doesn't mean he agrees with things. He spends his life in front of a video game and sometimes manages to cream the machine. His favorite hobby is winding up Jerry, but I know that he would die for him. What would he be without his big bro? Anything he wanted probably, just as I am now that I've moved away from my sister. David bites his nails, and when his fingernails are down to the quick, he starts in on his toenails. If he had nails anywhere else—his nose, his elbows, his knees—he'd bite those, too, you can count on it. He does it in silence. It's great having a kid who never cries, I'm not complaining, but it's a bit scary sometimes. I like it when he scratches his head, pretending to think. I'm forty-three and recently I've started to imitate him. As I said before: nowadays, parents imitate their kids. Do you know a better way of staying young? David is a little monkey: grouchy, scrawny, pale, irritable, and misanthropic. He reminds me of my father. Maybe he is my father! Jerry's my mother and David's my father.

"MOM, DAD, COME AND GIMME A BIG HUG!"

"Oh God, David," Jerry sounds alarmed, "the old man's lost it."

David looks at me and frowns but says nothing, as usual. We've just reached the 105th floor.

8:50

WHAT THEY DON'T KNOW BUT I NOW KNOW (WHICH DOESN'T make me any superior, it's simply hindsight) is that the Boeing destroyed all the exits: the stairwells are blocked, the elevators melted; Carthew and his two sons are utterly trapped in a furnace.

Signed: Mr. Know-it-all (in French, *Monsieur je-sais-tout*)

The Tour Montparnasse was inaugurated in 1974, at about the same time as the World Trade Center: 26 acres; each floor 21,500 square feet; 1.1 million square feet of office space; 320,000 square feet of shopping; 170,000 square feet of storage space; 1,000,000 square feet of communal areas, 220,000 square feet of specialized offices, 1,850 parking spaces. Width: 104 feet. twenty-five elevators and 7,200 windows. Weight: 130,000 tons. Foundations: 56 piles running to 230 feet below the forecourt, straddling four Métro lines.

This is why, at 8:50 A.M., the building scares me stiff. Since September 11, I see the Tour Montparnasse very differently, I can tell you: as a spaceship, a rocket about to take off, as the last pin standing in a bowling lane. Did you know that when the Maine-Montparnasse project was first announced, President Georges Pompidou wanted to build two identical towers? For a long time it was in the cards, then he gave up on the idea.

At the Lycée Montaigne, discipline was the enemy; we thought education was like military indoctrination; the endless, droning classes, the murky depths of capitalist democracy. Insubordination was more romantic. I admired the exploits of Action Direct on TV. They were free, they blew up things, kidnapped pot-bellied capitalists. Terrorist Nathalie Ménigon was sexier than Minister of Universities Alice Saunier-Séïté. At school, the coolest thing you could wear was a PLO scarf, but I was dressed in Burberry—talk about a rebel. Terrorism was a lot more glamorous than next Friday's history quiz. I should have run away, joined the underground movement, but the heating in squats was not up to the standards of my mother's apartment. At the Lycée Louis-le-Grand, I began poring over revolutionary manifestos while still keeping my grades up. That way, I could win on all fronts: I wouldn't get beaten up by the police, I wouldn't wind up in a maximum security prison, but I could quote Situationist Raoul Vaneigem and seem cool. It was a Canada Dry revolution: it looked rebellious, I looked like a rebel, but I wasn't a rebel. One day, an American journalist would come up with an acronym for the bourgeois bohemians: he called them "BoBos." I was getting ready to be a RiRe: a "rich rebel."

8:51

A STROKE OF LUCK (IF YOU CAN CALL IT THAT): ON THE 105TH floor, I get a signal on the cell phone. I call Mary at home.

"Hello?"

"Mary? It's Carthew. Sorry about all the coughing, but the boys are fine, we're going to do our best to get out of here."

"Carthew? Why are you whispering? What are you talking about?"

"There's been an accident, but I've told the boys that it's a theme park ride. Turn on the TV, you'll see what I mean."

Silence, not a sound. I hear a television being turned on, then a piercing scream: "Oh Lord, tell me this isn't happening. Carthew, don't tell me you're up there!"

"Shit, you're the one who told me to get the kids up early so they didn't get out of their school routine! I'd rather be somewhere else, I swear. I saw it, Mary, I SAW that fucking airplane crash right under us! It's starting to get hot and there's smoke everywhere, but the kids are OK, hang on, Jerry wants a word."

"Mom?"

"Oh, honey are you alright? You're not hurt? Look after your little brother for me, OK?"

"Mom, this ride is awesome, the place really stinks. Here's Dave."

". . ."

"David?"

"Kof kof *(he coughs).* Mom, Jerry won't lend me his camera!"

"Hi Mary, it's Carthew. Try and find out if they're sending in a rescue team, we can't get through to the lobby from here. We've had no fucking instruction on how to evacuate! Call me back. Later!"

We're still in the neon-lit stairwell following the herd down the stairs like lambs being led to the slaughter. Solzhenitsyn compared those exiled to the gulags to lambs. Baaa. What a stupid damn idea, bringing the kids here, they were bored shitless, they were as bored as I was. All these chores we put ourselves through thinking it's for the best. . . . Now, we're being punished for not sleeping in. Look at them, all these early risers in their shirts and ties, freshly shaven, the overperfumed working girls, the disciples of the *Wall Street Journal.* . . . They'd all have been better off staying in bed.

"You OK, kids? Keep your napkins over your nose and mouth, and don't touch the rails, they're really hot."

In the silence, the herd swells. At each floor we're joined by a traumatized legion in gray suits and pink pantsuits. We step over the tiles from the false ceilings obstructing the passage. The heat is suffocating. Sometimes someone gives his neighbor a hand, or cries, but most say nothing; they cough, they hope.

8:52

My parents met each other in the Basque country, but quickly left to study in America. Nowadays, we've forgotten how many French graduates were drawn to American universities, especially the business schools. So my father headed off to Harvard to do his MBA (as George W. Bush would do later), my mother went with him and used her time to get a master's in history at Mount Holyoke. Nineteen fifties America: like a black and white documentary. The dream reached out to the rest of the Western world. Long Cadillacs with fins, extra large ice creams, buttered popcorn at the movies, Eisenhower reelected: magical symbols of perfect happiness. This was the America that kept its promises, the country of Cockaigne described by the handsome, tanned actor and director Philippe Labro. At the time, dissent was insignificant. Nobody said McDonald's was fascist. Dad laughed at Bob Hope's jokes on TV. People went bowling. Middle-class kids were inventing globalization. They believed in America; to them it personified modernity, efficiency, freedom. Ten years later, this same generation voted for Valéry Giscard d'Estaing because he was young like JFK. Brilliant, energetic, no-bullshit guys. At last we'd be rid of the burden of our European education. Go all out. Be direct. Go straight to the point. In the United States, the first question you're asked is "Where are you from?" because everyone is from somewhere else. Then they say: "Nice to meet you." Because it's nice to meet new people. In the United States, when someone invites you over, you can help yourself from the fridge without asking your hostess's permission. I remember phrases from that period I often heard at home: "put your money where your mouth is," "big is beautiful," "back-seat driver" (my favorite; Mom used it when we were getting on her nerves from the back of the car); "take it easy," "relax," "gimme a break," "you're overreacting," "for God's sake." The capitalist utopia was just as crazy as the communist utopia, but its violence was covert. It won the Cold War because of its image: of course people were dying of starvation in America as they were in Russia, but those who were dying of starvation in America were free to do so.

All this was before 1968: the Beatles still had short hair. I remember my folks used to say that America was ten years ahead of France. Even the French Revolution happened thirteen years after theirs! If you wanted to know the future, all you had to do was keep your eyes glued to this idyllic country. Dad read the *Herald Tribune, Time,* and *Newsweek,* and kept *Playboy* hidden in his desk drawer. CNN didn't exist yet, but *Time* magazine, with its red-framed cover, was like a four-color process CNN. My mother got a scholarship to travel around the States on a Greyhound bus. She told me about the sea breeze, the excitement of the open road, the motels, the Buicks, the drive-ins, the drugstores, the diners, all those radio stations with names that began with "W." The whole world eyed America enviously, because you always look enviously at your own future. May '68 did not come from the East: there was a lot of talk about Trotsky and Engels, but the overriding influence was Western. I'm convinced that the roots of May '68 lay in the USA, not the USSR. It was an overpowering urge to say "fuck you" to old-fashioned bourgeois morality. The revolution of May '68 wasn't anti-capitalist, in fact it definitively ushered in the consumer society; the main difference between our generation and that of our parents was that they demonstrated *in favor* of globalization! I grew up in the decade that followed, in the benevolent shadow of the Star-Spangled Banner floating on the moon and posters of Charles Schulz's Snoopy. Films were released earlier in the U.S. than they were in France; Dad used to bring back all the spinoff toys when he went on business trips: a *Muppet Show* lunchbox, *Star Wars* merchandise, Slime, an *E.T.* doll. . . . It was during those years, the years of my amnesiac childhood, that the Spectacle of America seduced the rest of the world.

I hope America will always be ten years ahead of us: that would mean the Tour Montparnasse still has ten years.

8:53

FROM THE 104TH FLOOR, THROUGH THE CLOUD OF BLACK SMOKE, I can make out the crowd rushing toward the sea. A human torrent gushing from the building. What are they waiting for to organize the evacuation? Nobody's told us what to do. We're in the stairwell by Cantor Fitzgerald when the smoke becomes unbearable: poisonous, dense, sticky, and black like oil (which, of course, is what it is). The heat, too, makes us turn back. The stockbroker couple fall into the arms of their soot-covered colleagues. The whole floor is drenched: the sprinklers are spitting out a safety drizzle. Everyone gets to have a shower. Water is pouring down the stairs. David splashes in the stream.

"Careful! You're going to slip and break your neck."

Jerry holds his hand.

"OK, it was a trick. We obviously weren't supposed to go downstairs. Jerry, let's go back up, whaddya think?"

"Mmghpfgmmz."

I can't really make out what he's saying through his blackened napkin, but he nods. So we turn around. Jerry's my favorite on odd days, David on even. So today I prefer Jerry, particularly because he believes every word when I tell him this is just a game, a piece of trickery, whereas David is silent but understands everything. We retrace our steps, the faces we meet ever more terrified; in front of us a man starts to giggle nervously swinging a busted fire hose (some of the pipes must have been burst by the plane). The tension mounts; we'll have to play a tight game. I deserve an Academy Award! I hold a child's hand in each of mine and play the part of father courage.

"I think it's a great initiative to have full-scale fire drills like this. That way when there's a real fire, people will be prepared. It's a good way to learn. Just now, for example, that was to teach us that when there's a fire, you shouldn't go downstairs, but actually get as high as possible. It's an educational game."

Then, suddenly, David starts to speak, staring at the river running down the steps.

"Dad, remember when we went to the rodeo in Dallas, and the cowboy got hurt falling off a bull?"

"Um, yeah, yeah . . ."

"Well, you told us that he wasn't hurt, that guy, that he was supposed to fall and that it had all been worked out, that he was a professional stuntman and everything, but on TV the next day we saw the cowboy in a wheelchair and on the news they said that he was quarterpleenic."

"Quadraplegic, Dave, the word is 'quadraplegic.'"

"Yeah, that's it: the cowboy guy, he was quadrapleezic."

I preferred it when David didn't say a word. Jerry chimed in; it's not a mutiny, it's a revolution:

"Dad, you don't have to tell us all the time that everything bad is pretend. Let's face it, this time it's for real."

David, Jerry, my little boys, how quickly you've grown up.

"OK, OK, kids, maybe I'm wrong, maybe it's not a game, but

we should go back upstairs calmly anyway. The rescue services are on their way, so stay cool."

As I said this, I rolled my eyes as though I didn't believe a word of it and muttered loudly as if I were talking to myself:

"Just my luck, if the kids think this thing's for real, I'm gonna look a complete jerk in front of the other players. Oh, well, never mind . . ."

David, my baby. Tough guy. A real Texan, I swear; suddenly I feel really old. We're back on the 105th floor. The herd vacillates in this freshly painted prison with its yellow walls. Terrified faces hesitate between up and down. They're deliberating: die quickly, die slowly? Panic overcomes me as I listen to the fire alarms from the floors below, which are obviously still working and are deafening us. The racket is terrible, and it's getting hotter by the second. Then, suddenly, after about thirty attempts, the cell-phone network is back: Candace's phone is ringing. She's probably asleep. I leave a message on her answering machine.

"I know you won't believe this, but I love you. When you wake up in the morning you'll understand why I'm being all corny."

I whisper again so the kids can't hear.

"It doesn't look good, babe. I've been such a fool. If we get out of here, I'm going to marry you. I have to hang up because I need to try and breathe for the three of us. Love you. Carthew."

8:54

FIFTEEN YEARS AGO, I VISITED WINDOWS ON THE WORLD MYSELF, but not at breakfast time. It was late one night in July 1986. The lights of the World Trade Center appeared to me like the evening star. I was twenty years old and working as an intern in the analysis department at the New York office of Crédit Lyonnais (95 Wall Street). During my placement, my principal preoccupation was how to sleep at the office without Philippe Souviron—a friend of my father's who ran the New York office—finding out. In those days, after midnight Windows on the World, under the truly arrogant name the Greatest Bar on Earth, became a meeting place for people you'd happily punch in the face. The Greatest Bar on Earth had started organizing theme nights every Wednesday: Latino, beatbox, electric boogie with DJs and a whole ecosystem of arrogant little assholes like me, but, hey, the kitchens were closed, the restaurant was closed and a jacket was still required. I remember the U-shaped red bar and the sneering bartenders. The guy in the middle was on good terms with me, though, because I'd accidentally dropped him a huge tip (mistaking a twenty-dollar bill for a five).

He served my double Jack Daniel's with ice piled to the top of the glass and two short straws which I'd quite happily have used for something else if I'd had any blow. The tables of the Greatest Bar on Earth were staggered over several levels, as in Le Ciel de Paris, for the same reason—so that all the customers could admire the colossal, breathtaking, spectacular view, which, sadly, was cut into sections, since the soaring picture windows were divided into slivers three feet wide. The towers, the brainchild of Yamasaki, the Japanese architect, who was keen to use exterior pillars that had the span of human shoulders, looked like the interior of a vast prison. The Japanese was deceitful: the vertical steel pillars that ran the length of the towers from top to bottom blocked my view like the bars of a cell (in fact, the only things to survive the collapse were the parallel metal stakes found planted at Ground Zero, like a rusted portcullis among the ruins of a thirteenth-century fortress after a bloody battle, or the beams of a gothic cathedral razed by barbarians).

Even so, I drank whiskey, leaning into the abyss, swaying prophetically, getting drunk among the blinking helicopters in a place that no longer exists. Is it possible that the man standing there so full of himself fifteen years ago is me? Hemmed in by windows, we danced to Madonna's "Into the Groove." I spilled whiskey on the dresses of tipsy girls from Riverside Drive who made fun of the "bridge and tunnel crowd" (their name for those from the outer boroughs who had to take a bridge or tunnel to get to Manhattan). Back then, I dreamed of a future like Donald Trump, Mike Milken, Nick Leeson, pockets stuffed with cash and the world at my feet. That night at Windows on the World I gave it everything I had, but the past is dead and nothing can prove that what no longer exists ever did exist.

The night I went there, New York was overcast, but the tower pierced the clouds. The Greatest Bar on Earth floated on a sea of cotton. To the right, the rich could look out at the lights of Brooklyn reflected in the sea, to the left you could see nothing except the same white, cotton carpet you can see from an airplane window during a flight. The World Trade Center was striped: imagine a pair of columns 1,350 feet tall. The DJ blasted out dry ice, a cold white mist that glided across the dance floor. We were dancing on a freezing flying carpet.

Me and my partner in crime back then, a guy called Alban de Clermont-Tonnerre, were waiting for a promise: some girl called Lee he'd picked up in a singles bar—one of the famous Second Avenue pick-up bars the French found so exciting. He'd got her to agree to a threesome, but she hadn't shown up yet.

"Aaaw . . . all dressed up and been stood up!"

Alban was pretty miserable, and I wasn't much better. Our potential threesome seemed, like the whiskey, to be on the rocks. Even so, a couple of Jack Daniel's later I found them wrapped around each other by those windows, which have since been shattered. They were making out, and I made the most of it, copping a feel of Lee's nipples, which were hard under her indigo dress. She jerked round to look and what did she see? A big, ham-fisted, sallow guy in a Prince of Wales check suit far too big for him; a pale, pimply little guy with long greasy hair and a seriously deformed chin who was about as charming as a tubercular gargoyle. Serial killers were a new thing back then, and I looked a lot like one. A death's-head mask in a dead restaurant.

"Who is this guy? Are you crazy? Get your fucking hands off me!"

When I saw Alban's embarrassed expression, I realized the threesome clearly hadn't been in the cards, so he'd gone back to a twosome. I didn't really care: she was dark-haired, a bit tubby, really—nothing to write home about—she worked so hard she didn't have time for a serious relationship; that's why she hung out in singles bars where she knew the only guys she'd ever meet were frustrated dweebs like us. Here I was playing gooseberry again; later I'd go home drunk in a yellow contraption driven by a Haitian voodoo master. I went back to the dance floor, now disappeared. I probably looked a bit depressed; in fact I was paralyzed with shyness. The chicks rubbed up against the Brooks Brothers shirts of millionaire stockbrokers. I had another buddy back then, Bernard-Louis, a bit of a playboy—all the girls called him Belou. Belou this and Belou that. I decided to hang out with him. Not being in love was exhausting; you constantly had to work at being attractive, and the competition was stiff. It was creepy, needing so desperately to be loved. It was at that moment I think that I decided to be famous.

8:55

SMOKE STINGS THE KIDS' EYES.

"Put the napkin over your eyes as well—eyes, nose and mouth—cover your whole face, do you read me?"

Jerry and David, dressed like Casper the Friendly Ghost, napkins over the heads, as the blue sky of Armageddon brought the first tears to our eyes. Thank God the napkins mean the boys didn't see the human torches on 106: two bodies in flames near the elevator doors, skin red and black, lidless eyes, hair turned to ashes, faces peeling away, covered in blisters fused to the melted linoleum. From the movement of their chests we could tell they were still alive. The rest of their bodies are still as statues.

I had to pull myself together. It was becoming difficult to perform the simplest of tasks: breathing. If only because of the stench, which was unbearable. The dense smoke stank of melted rubber, burning plastic, charred flesh. The cloying scent of airplane fuel, sickly and terrifying, powdered bones and human flesh turned to ashes. A mixture of toxic waste, pungent diesel and the crematorium; the sort of thing you might smell driving past a factory, the sort of smell that makes you hold your breath and step on the gas. If death has a smell, it must be this. Rubble from a collapsed ceiling blocks the way back up to Windows. At least ten of us set about moving a concrete slab. In the end we manage to squeeze through to get back to the roof of this city in the sky.

On the 107th floor, the waitress and the two brothers who work in the kitchen have smashed a window with a pedestal table (helpful hint: to break a large picture window, do not use an chair or an iMac. The best solution is to run at it using the cast iron leg of a pedestal table as a battering ram). At 1,350 feet up, they lean out the windows waving white tablecloths. The murky smoke is thick as blotting paper soaked in axle grease. Even so, there are gaps through which I can pick out images of the outside world. What fascinates me most are the sheets of paper floating in the blue: files, photocopies, urgent memos, duplicated company listings on letterhead paper, registered mail, confidential files, portfolios, 4-color laser prints, self-adhesive envelopes, Jiffy bags, printed labels, piles of stapled contracts, plastic binders, multicolored Post-it notes, invoices in triplicate, graphs and charts and balance sheets, all this scattered paperwork, this stationery on the wing, and the comparative magnitude of our signaling. These thousands of fluttering pieces of paper remind me of the showers of paper so dear to New Yorkers during Broadway tickertape parades. What are we celebrating today?

Genesis 11:4:

"And they said, Go to, let us build ourselves a city and a tower, whose top may reach into heaven; and let us make us a name . . ."

8:56

EVERYONE KNOWS PRECISELY WHERE THEY WERE ON SEPTEMBER 11, 2001. Personally, I was in the basement of my publisher Grasset, giving an interview for *Culture Pub* at 2:56 P.M. French time when the presenter, Thomas Hervé, was informed via cell phone that an airplane had just flown into one of the World Trade Center towers. At the time, we both thought it was a small tourist plane and went on with the interview. We were talking about cultural marketing. How do you publish a book? Should you play by the rules? To what extent? Are television, marketing, and advertising the enemies of art? Is the word necessarily in opposition to the image? At the time, I had just agreed to host a weekly literary TV show on a cable network. I was attempting to justify the contradictions in my role as writer/critic/presenter:

"The role of books is to record what cannot be seen on television. . . . Literature is under threat, we have to fight for it, this is war. . . . People who enjoy reading and writing are more and more scarce, that's why we have to hedge our bets. . . . Use every weapon at our disposal to defend literature. . . ."

When suddenly someone from the publishers came to tell

us that a second plane had flown into the other World Trade Center tower. My litero-military perorations suddenly seemed ridiculous. I remember reciting aloud a simple mathematical (though hardly Euclidian) equation:

1 plane = 1 accident
2 planes = 0 accident.

Thomas and I agreed that my prime-time struggle-to-defend-the-epistolary-arts-against-media-repression could wait. We went upstairs to the office of Claude Dalla Torre—one of the PR people, and the only person with a working television. TF1 was rebroadcasting LCI, which was rebroadcasting CNN: we watched as the second plane headed straight for the intact tower; the other tower looked like an Olympic torch, like the tornado on the poster for *Twister*. The inexperienced TV news anchors seemed disbelieving. They were reluctant to stick their necks out, content to let the live feed run uninterrupted, terrified of saying something that would be on every blooper reel for the next thirty years. Claude's office quickly filled up—at Grasset, any excuse is a good excuse not to work. Each had a different reaction to what was happening.

Narcissistic: "Fuck—I was just up there a month ago!"

Statistical: "My God, how many people are trapped in there? The death toll must be 20,000!"

Paranoid: "Jesus, well, since I look like an Arab, I'm bound to get stopped by the cops every five minutes for the next couple of weeks."

Anxious: "We've got to call our friends over there, make sure they're all right."

Laconic: "Well, this is no joke."

Marketing: "This is going to be great for the ratings! We should buy space on LCI."

Bellicose: "Fuck! This is it, it's the Third World War."

Security conscious: "They need to put cops on all the planes and bulletproof doors on the cockpits."

Nostradamus: "You see? I told you this would happen, I even wrote it."

Media savvy: "Shit, I have to get over to Europe 1 and give my reaction."

Knee-jerk Anti-American: "This is what happens when you try and control the world."

Fatalistic: "It was bound to happen some day or other."

As the minutes passed, as we watched, hypnotized, again and again as the airliner headed straight for the tower (it didn't hesitate, it *zeroed in*, as if drawn by a magnet, to be swallowed in a black and orange fireball by the tower), the jokes petered out, faces grew longer, people slumped into chairs, cell phones rang, the bags under our eyes deepened. The extent of the tragedy gradually began to weigh on our shoulders. We became hunchbacks. We were just beginning to shut up, in other words, when a third plane crashed into the Pentagon. Fucking hell: the sky was literally falling on them. You know what happened next: with the collapse first of the South Tower and then, at 4:30 P.M. French time, the North Tower, the atmosphere turned to global fear. I was white as a sheet, I don't even remember whether I said goodbye to Françoise Verny as I started down the stairs. I must have walked home. Somewhere on the rue Saint-André-des-Arts, my phone rang. It was Eric Laurrent, a fellow novelist published by Les Editions de Minuit who'd just finished a book set in the United States (*Do Not Touch:* it's a title I recommend you disobey). He was looking for work and had just offered his services on my TV program. I don't know why, but he wasn't aware of what had happened.

"Sorry, Eric, I'm feeling a little weird. . . . It's been a bizarre day. . . ."

"Really, what's the matter? Are you okay?"

"Um, the um, the World Trade Center towers collapsed, there's airplanes crashing into everything, the Pentagon is on fire, you know . . ."

"Yeah, yeah, very funny . . . Seriously, though, if there is a job going, I'm up for it, I'm up shit creek financially."

He was justified in being unable to believe me. I had a credibility problem; everything I said was unreliable, even the truth. Just because I made a fortune criticizing the rich. Even when I said "I love you," nobody believed me. Next I phoned my daughter: I just needed to know where she was. I couldn't get hold of Chloë; her mom had turned off her cell phone. I had to wait half an hour before the nanny called me back: she was at the puppet theater watching *The Three Little Pigs.* I was lucky. No Boeing smashed into the Jardin de Luxembourg that day. On the phone, Chloë told me the story:

"It's all about this wolf and he wants to eat the little pigs but the pigs build this house with bricks and he can't, the wolf can't eat them."

And I thought: it's wrong to indoctrinate young children with such lies.

8:57

Concerto for Coughs, Sneezes, Throat Clearing, and Strangulation

STRANGE THAT NOT A SINGLE AVANT-GARDE COMPOSER THOUGHT of the idea. Not even John Cage? Even though his name was perfect for the part. We're performing a concerto for coughs in a crystal cage. I think back to a trip to Réunion, when Mary and I took the boys to see an active volcano. It felt like I was back there: the sulfur fumes, the suffocating heat, Jerry and David coughing and sputtering. The World Trade Center was an erupting volcano. Back in Windows on the World (107th floor), I can think of only one solution: block the ventilation shafts with our jackets, close the fire doors, seal the doorways with wet towels, upend the tables against the ventilation grilles, and wait for the rescue services. In the restaurant, the Risk Water Group are huddled in the northwest corner (there's less smoke). Some cling to the columns and stick their heads out the windows. There's room to squeeze in three, maybe four people if we hoist ourselves up. Standing on the table, I lift Jerry and David in turn so they can get a breath of fresh air. In the vast room and in front of the bar smoke creeps across the floor like ground water.

Customers are beginning to understand they're trapped. The receptionist and the head chef are barraged with questions. What's the evacuation procedure? Haven't you got a plan of the building? They almost come to blows trying to make it clear that they're just as much in the shit as we are. The chubby Puerto Rican waitress is called Lourdes; she helps me hoist the children toward the windows.

"Don't worry," she says, "they'll come and get us. I was here in February '93 when the bomb went off. Hear the police copters?"

"But how are they gonna get us out of here? It's too dangerous, they can't come near the building."

"Well, in '93, they airlifted a lot of people from the roof."

"Dammit you're right! Gimme a hug!"

I put my arms around her and then collect the boys.

"Lourdes, come with me. It was a mistake trying to go downstairs earlier, we should have gone up! Come on, kids, back to the game: everyone up on the roof."

And here we are again, the four of us heading for the smoke-filled stairway. Revived from the fresh air, Jerry and David play Beetlejuice with their napkins. But the black security guard stops us going back into the stairwell.

"It's impossible, the whole place is on fire."

"Is there some other way up to the roof?"

"Anthony," says Lourdes, "remember '93? We've got to get to the roof. They're gonna come and airlift us off the roof, they might be waiting for us already."

Anthony thinks. His arm has second-degree burns, but he

thinks. His shirt is in tatters, but he thinks. And I now know what he's thinking: it's fucked, but I can't let them down.

"OK, follow me."

We fall in behind him, weaving through the maze of kitchens and offices in the highest restaurant in the world. He avoids the blocked stairwells, squeezes through corridors crammed with crates of French wine, and gets us to climb up a steel ladder. Jerry and David are having a ball. With white napkins over their faces they look like highwaymen, or like a couple of Ukrainian peasant women. We arrive on the 108th floor. Clearly we're not the only ones with the idea. Soon there are about twenty of us trying to get to the roof. Frantically, I dial 911 to alert the rescue services. Jerry asks why I keep punching today's date into my cell phone: 911, 911, 911. Nine Eleven.

"It's a coincidence, honey. Just a coincidence."

"What's a coindesense?" asks David.

"It's when things happen all at the same time that seem like they're connected and you think it's on purpose but it's not on purpose, that's what coincidence means, huh, Dad?"

"Yeah, that's right. It's just chance, but gullible people think it's an omen. Like, for instance, some people might think that the fact today's date is the same as the emergency services number is like a secret message. That someone's trying to tell us something. But that's just bullshit, it's obviously a coincidence."

"Is 'bullshit' a bad word?" asks David.

"Yeah," says Jerry.

"You shouldn't say 'bullshit,' Dad, it's not nice."

8:58

THE FIRE REGULATIONS AT LE CIEL DE PARIS ARE EXACTLY AS THEY were before September 11: exit in a calm and orderly fashion via the stairs. And if the stairs are damaged, full of smoke, white hot, like an oven? Well, um, wait calmly to be burned, asphyxiated, or crushed to death. OK, fine, thanks. The way up to the roof is still sealed off to stop smart kids coming and partying at night. It happened: a couple of years back, a gang of squatters organized a picnic on the roof of the tower. Since then, the movements of every young alcoholic are carefully monitored.

"In any case," said a member of the security staff, "if a 747 flew into the Tour Montparnasse, it would be sliced in two straight away so the question of evacuation wouldn't arise."

Well, that's reassuring. To get my mind off the subject I think about a serious semantic problem that has occurred to me: what verb should one use for parking a plane in a building? Not "to land," since there is no longer any question of reaching land (the same problem arises with the French "*atterrir,*" which presupposes the presence of *terre* beneath the wheels). I propose "to skyscrape." Example: "Ladies and gentlemen, this is your captain speaking. We are now approaching our destination and will soon be skyscraping in Paris. Please stow your tray tables, return your seats to the upright position, and fasten your seatbelts. We hope you've enjoyed your flight with Air France and regret that we will not have the pleasure of seeing you on our airline, or indeed anywhere else again."

That said, you can visit the roof during the day. Unlike the roof of the North Tower of the World Trade Center (inaccessible), the roof of the Tour Montparnasse is open to the public for a fee of €8.00. You can take the elevator to the 56th floor with a handful of Japanese tourists dressed in black and the mustachioed security guard, who is wearing a navy blue blazer with gold buttons. (When I was a kid, I was dressed like that, itchy flannel trousers and a sailor's blazer, and I made much the same angry face.) On the 56th floor, you visit a little exhibition about Paris, and already you can enjoy the panoramic views. My gaze plummets through the picture windows to Montparnasse Cemetery looking for Baudelaire's grave, a white pebble in a garden of stone. On the left, the Jardin de Luxembourg, the distant childhood I try to prolong by remaining stock still, as if staying in the same place geographically might somehow stop time. I'm not young anymore, simply geostationary. A dismal cafeteria (the Café Belvédère) serves goblets of hot liquid to tired provincials. To get to the roof, you have to brave a stairway that smells of bleach (memories of swimming pools, rowdy lessons, toweling swimming trunks and smelly feet). Out of breath, I climb the last steps, my efforts rewarded by stenciled numbers on the wall indicating the altitude ("201 meters, 204 meters, 207 meters"). A metal gate opens onto the sky. Wind whistles through the bars. From here, you can see planes take off from Orly. In the middle of the concrete roof, a white circle has been painted for helicopters to skyscrape. If I wanted to, I could throw things into the void onto passersby. I might be arrested for vandalism or attempted murder or malicious wounding occasioning involuntary manslaughter, or dangerous schizophrenia or inexplicable hysteria or frenzied panic. Pink mist, far off, over the Sacré-Coeur. A billboard attempts a pun: LA VUE PARISIENNE. This is mine: my name is Frédéric Belvédère. I go downstairs to Le Ciel de Paris. A similar restaurant exists in Berlin at the summit of the TV-Turm on Alexanderplatz, and that one spins around like a record. In the seventies, the modern world desperately wanted to dine in a skyscraper, lunch in the stratosphere, eating at altitude was chic—I don't know why. On the floor with the "panoramic exhibition," a screening room shows old aerial pictures of Paris to a depressing flute soundtrack. The tape wows and flutters. People in parkas walk around looking bored. Lovers force themselves to kiss full on the mouth despite their breath. A child yawns; I imitate him; perhaps he is me.

And then, instinctively, for no particular reason I turn to look at Denfert-Rochereau, and that's when I see a human ribbon made up of thousands of individuals, a river of hair piled up round the square. The largest anti-war demonstration for fifty years; it is February 15, 2003. Yesterday, the U.S. took on France in the UN Security Council. The President of the United States, like his father, wants to go to war with Iraq; the President of France does not agree. Anti-Americans slug it out with Francophobes. Televised insults are hurled liberally on both sides of the Atlantic. At the foot of my tower, the mammoth protest march stretches from the Place Denfert to the Bastille—200,000 people marching in the cold along the Boulevard Saint-Michel, beneath the freezing sky of the Boulevard Saint-Germain. . . . On the same day, the same number of marchers are saying the same thing on the streets of New York. I take the elevator down to join them. Am I a coward, an appeaser, an anti-Semite, a cheese-eating surrender monkey, as the American newspapers say? Turning back toward the smoked glass monolith from which rays of sunlight ricochet, I decide to rename the Tour Montparnasse. In contrast to the Twin Towers, I shall name it the Lonely Tower. This curved rectangle, the shape of a cracked almond at each end, that ridiculous, forlorn beacon surges from between the couscous restaurants and the merguez vendors. Along rue du Départ I meet lots of North Africans in front of a wall that has been painted by Walt Disney Pictures acclaiming *The Jungle Book 2*. Baloo the bear is dancing with Mowgli across ten meters of façade among the stale fat of shish kabobs. The protesters brandish banners: STOP THE WAR. The Disney movie takes place in the Indian jungle colonized by the British. But there is a moral to the book that is absent from the cartoon: "Now in the jungle there's something more than the law of the jungle." Come back, Kipling, they've all gone mad!

8:59

Oh shit, the tall red-haired guy has flipped. He's screaming at the top of his lungs, but you can't make out a word. He's sweating like a pig. To stop the kids freaking out, I decide to try the theme park story again. I ask Lourdes to look after them, giving her a wink so she'll play along.

"Sorry, Lourdes, could I ask you a favor? The thing is, my kids refuse to believe this is a theme park ride—they've never heard of Tower Inferno—anyway, could you look after them for a couple of minutes while I go and check out the way to the roof with Anthony, OK? Boys, you behave yourselves, promise?"

"Promise."

"And don't pay any attention to that guy shouting, he's just an actor, and not a very good one."

"Why is your name Lourdes?"

"Shut up, Dave!" says Jerry.

"Boys, boys," says Lourdes, "you'll have to cool it a bit, because I work here and I can tell you usually they don't let kids your age on this ride because you're not regulation height, so if I were you I wouldn't kick up a fuss, do I make myself clear?"

Anthony takes the red-haired guy by the shoulders and talks to him very calmly. They're crouched in the mirrored hallway. Columns of foul smoke snake round the elevator shafts like black ivy.

"It's OK, it'll be OK. Don't worry, it's gonna be OK."

He keeps saying this until he calms down. The red-haired guy is bawling he's so scared; he's lost his nerve. I try to join in:

"What's your name?"

"Jeffrey."

"Look, Jeffrey, we've all gotta stick together, OK? Don't worry, everything'll be fine. Just keep cool."

"OH GOD, OH GOD IT'S ALL MY FAULT I WAS THE ONE WHO ARRANGED THE WORKING BREAKFAST I DON'T WANNA DIE I'M SORRY I'M SORRY OH GOD I'M A JERK I'M SORRY I'M SORRY I'M SO SCARED OH GOD HAVE MERCY!"

I look around to see if the kids are freaking out too: but no, they're holding up. They've got their hands over their ears so they can't hear Jeffrey screaming: "I'VE GOTTA GET OUT!" It's something Lourdes showed them. By a stairway blocked with pipes Anthony takes me to the 109th floor. We walk through rooms full of huge multicolored machines, between cooling turbines, boilers, and the elevator machinery. Clearly everyone else has had the same idea. After all, what choice do we have? Downstairs is a furnace, death from burns or asphyxiation is inevitable. Our only hope is to get out via the roof. Little by little we're joined by a hundred people; they spread out, looking for pockets of fresh air. Groups of people take their heads in their hands; sit or stand; climb on tables in an effort to breathe; throw metal lockers through the windows to let oxygen in (yeah, it works with a metal locker too).

Bunches of people welded together, propping each other up, holding hands, consoling each other, coughing.

"There's only one set of stairs to the roof," says Anthony. "I've got a key—all the security guards have one."

We're standing in front of a red door marked EMERGENCY EXIT. I don't yet know how much I will come to despise that door.

On the floor below, Lourdes is keeping up a running banter with my two sons, turning her head this way and that like she's watching the Williams sisters play tennis.

"I'd rather be in school," says David.

"No way, this is just too cool," says Jerry.

"Cooler than high school?" says David.

"Yeah, sure," says Jerry.

"Yeah, but it's really hot," says David.

"You said it," says Jerry. "Feels like being in a sauna."

"What's a sauna?" says David.

"A sauna is like a bathroom that's really hot to make you sweat," says Lourdes.

"But what's it for?" says David.

"It's supposed to make you thin," says Lourdes.

"You should go to one sometime," says David.

"Shut up, Dave," says Jerry. "You're not funny."

"Shut up yourself! I am too funny, even Lourdes is laughing. . . ." says David.

Lourdes is doubled up, she's laughing so hard she's crying. She takes out a packet of Kleenex to wipe away the tears.

"You think we'll be on TV?"

" 'Course, dumbass," says Jerry, "we're probably live on like a dozen channels right now."

"Wow, cool!" says David.

"Da bomb," says Jerry.

"Pity you used up all the film in your camera," says David.

"Tell me about it, I'm pissed," says Jerry.

"Hey, your nose is bleeding," says David.

"Ah shit, not again," says Jerry.

And he puts his head back, stuffing his napkin against his nose. Lourdes gives him a tissue,

"Don't worry about him, Lourdes," says David. "He gets these all the time."

"Only when I'm angry," says Jerry.

"Like I said, all the time," says David.

9:00

Other eyewitness accounts? It's like being in an apocalyptic J. G. Ballard novel, except this is reality. Edmund McNally, CTO at Fiduciary, calls his wife, Liz, as the earth rumbles. He's coughing hard. Quickly, he recites his life insurance policies and employee bonus programs. He just has time to tell her that she's the whole world to him. He calls her right back to advise her to cancel a trip to Rome he had booked. On the 92nd floor, Damian Meehan telephones his brother Eugene, a firefighter in the Bronx: "It's pretty bad here," he shouts. "The elevators are gone." Peter Alderman, a broker at Bloomberg LP, sends an e-mail to his mother from his PDA; he mentions the smoke, then adds: "I'm scared." I think that by 9:00 A.M., that phrase sums up the general atmosphere. Following the surprise, the shock, the hope, after fifteen minutes all that remains is terror, a brute fear that clouds all judgment and turns legs to jelly.

This morning, I took my daughter to the Tour Montparnasse. Those who don't have children of three and a half skip straight to the next minute: they couldn't possibly understand.

First, I had to convince her that it was more interesting to go to the Tour Montparnasse than to the amusement park next door. In the end, we went to both. She insisted on running after the pigeons until they flew away, climbing over the concrete blocks, playing tightrope along the edge of the escalators. First tantrum, crying fit, negotiation, reconciliation. When she finally got bored with walking down the up escalator, I managed to drag her to the elevators. She cried because I didn't let her push the button for the 56th floor. She giggled when she felt the elevator move off, the pressure mounting against her eardrums. In Le Ciel de Paris, she gamboled between the legs of the waiters in their nylon uniforms. We took a table near the windows. I showed her the City of Light. She wanted to keep her furry jacket on. Second tantrum, crying fit, negotiation, reconciliation. Since children's lives aren't very dramatic, they make them theatrical. Anything is an excuse for dramatics, hysterics, screaming, joy, fits of laughter, furious foot-stamping. There's very little difference between a toddler's life and a Shakespeare play. If truth be told, my daughter is Sarah Bernhardt. She can move from utter despair to sublime happiness in the blink of an eye—a rare talent. The waitress (who's beginning to recognize me, since she sees me here every morning) offers her candy. She's ecstatic, her eyes dazzle, she blows kisses, puffing into the palm of her hand. The hot chocolate is too hot? Violent rage, brows knotted, sullen pout, lower lip stuck out in disgust. Nothing is bland when you're just discovering life. My daughter's life is intense. She sings "*Une souris verte qui courait dans l'herbe*" for the thirtieth time this morning. I can't stand that awful fucking nursery rhyme anymore. After a few minutes' silent contemplation of Paris, Chloë turns away from me, more interested in the dog at the next table. She goes to talk to him, nervously at first but relaxed after a minute. She shows him the view, explaining:

"It's very high. An' I'm on'y liddle."

The spaniel agrees. To celebrate this, she tries to tie a bow with his ears. I get up to go over and fetch her, apologizing to the dog's owners, who have noticed nothing.

"Your daughter is just adorable!"

"Thanks, but give it time, you'll change your mind."

"I WANT to stay with the DOG!"

Third tantrum, crying fit, negotiation, reconciliation. Deafened by the racket, the people at the next table do indeed change their minds. I try to buy her silence by offering her a Carambar.

"No, 'cos s'all sticky."

I'd like to do what my daughter does from time to time. The next time someone annoys me, whether on the set of a talk show or some reading panel, I swear, I'm going to burst into tears, scream and roll around on the floor. I'm sure this would be a very effective technique in politics, for example. "Vote for me, or I'll scream even louder." That's what we should have done with Robert Hue, the French Communist Party chief!

We finished our breakfast apart from the hot chocolate (by now too cold). On the way down in the elevator, my daughter smiled at me and whispered, "I love you, Daddy." I took her in my arms. I knew she was just trying to get me to forgive her for her unforgivable behavior in Le Ciel de Paris. Never mind: I accepted this gift. Once, when I had a raging toothache, I took a huge dose of morphine. It was astonishing, but less mind-blowing than this hug, my nose in her hair, pressed into the scent of mild almond shampoo, overwhelmed with gratitude.

9:01

YOU CAN MAKE THE TRIP HOLDING YOUR BREATH. TAKE A DEEP breath and dive into the smoke, keep your arms out in front of you, feel your way down the stairs, turn right after the bar, past the elevators and keep walking straight ahead to the north face. Climber's jargon: I feel like we're on an expedition at the top of the Himalayas with no breathing apparatus. Coming down quickly to check on the boys, despising myself for leaving them alone even for a minute. Lourdes was holding a blood-stained Kleenex.

"Damn! Your nosebleed come back?"

"It's okay, Dad, it'll stop in a sec."

"Raise your right arm and press against the nostril. Don't put your head back, otherwise it'll just keep running down your throat and it won't stop. Thanks, Lourdes. Were they well behaved?"

"Course they were, but just because I'm black doesn't mean you can assume I'm their nanny, OK?"

"But, uh . . . no, of course n—"

"Did Anthony find the way up to the roof?"

"Yeah. We'll head up soon as Jerry's nose stops bleeding. I hope you can hold your breath for sixty seconds."

How did I get to be a bastard? Was Mary suddenly less of a turn-on than the secretaries at Austin Maxi? When exactly did I go off the rails? When Jerry was born, when David was born? I think I lost it the day I looked in the mirror in my walk-in closet and realized I'd started dressing like my father. It had all happened so fast—job, marriage, kids. I didn't want this life anymore. I didn't want to become my father. When I was little I was ashamed of him when he insisted on wearing his Stetson in the street in Austin, just as Jerry is ashamed of me when I wear my Mets cap.

Paterfamilias is a full-time job; the problem is, I know fewer and fewer men who are prepared to take it on. We've been shown too many images of men who are free, poetic, and attractive, exhausted with pleasure; rock 'n' roll types running from their responsibilities straight into the arms of girls in dental-floss bikinis. How could anyone want to be like Lester Burnham when society idolizes Jim Morrison?

I like to watch Candace dance. She cranks up the volume on her stereo and sways and twirls barefoot on the rug; her hair wheels and she looks me straight in the eye as she takes off her T-shirt. . . . I think it's the most beautiful thing I know: Candace in her push-up bra on my king-size bed, dancing or painting her toenails. She bought a CD of "music to make love to," a collection of "lounge music," and every time she put it on, I knew I was a goner. . . . I miss her much more now that I'm not sure I'll ever see her again.

* * *

Come on, kids, come with Dad. Hold your breath, like in the swimming pool, OK? Take a deep breath and dive into the smoke, keep your arms out in front of you, past the elevators, turn left after the bar, and feel your way up the stairs . . .

On the 110th floor, Lourdes pointed out a poster to me: IT'S HARD TO BE DOWN WHEN YOU'RE UP. No comment.

The good thing about being single is that you don't have to cough to cover the splash when you take a dump.

One day, Mary brought a hand up to my face, her cold hand to the rosy cheek of her bashful lover. She told me I was her lover; I said no, I'm your husband; it just came out. It never occurred to me that one day I'd need someone else. A tear trickled from my left eye to warm her right hand. I knew that I would have a child with this woman. I was young, pure, manipulated maybe but utterly optimistic. Sincere. Alive. Dumb.

"Dad, I did a whole minute without breath, I beat my record!"

Jerry's timed himself all the way to the emergency exit on the roof.

"Dead easy, huh? I could do it standing on my head."

"Liar! I heard you coughing, that means you must have breathed."

"Not true—you're the one that cheated."

"Dad, tell him I didn't cheat, Dad!"

"Take it easy, kids, let's just sit down and wait for Anthony—he'll open this damn door for us. Okay?"

"Okay, but I didn't cheat."

"Did too."
"Did not."
"Did too."
"Did not."
"Did too."

I never thought that one day I'd come to enjoy their constant squabbles, that these sterile arguments would be like a mountain rescue team. Our kids are like St. Bernards. Jerry was sitting in the lotus position. He'd dried his tears, I smiled at him. Turn and turn about: now I was the one who felt like crying. Let's just say we were taking it in turns.

9:02

In the South Tower, the one that hadn't been damaged, the instructions were clear: do not evacuate. No way was anyone going to risk having a molten steel girder from the North Tower landing on their heads. So the security guards ordered anyone who came down to the lobby to go back up to their offices. As they did Stanley Praimnath. He went back up to the 81st floor, to his office with the Fuji Bank. And he looked out the window. At first, it was simply a gray arrow on the horizon. A plane passing behind the Statue of Liberty. Which grew slowly bigger. He had time to see the red marker on the fuselage: UNITED AIRLINES. Then the plane lifted its nose and headed straight for him. It was 9:02 A.M. Lousy day. Lousy fucking day.

As I took the Tour Montparnasse elevator again, I felt my stomach heave into my mouth. I should have taken the stairs to see what it's like to walk down 57 floors while the sky is on fire. But I'm a writer, not a stuntman, and my daughter would have started crying after five floors. I'll do it tomorrow morning.

* * *

At 9:02 and 54 seconds, United Airlines Flight 175, another Boeing 767, another Boston–Los Angeles flight, dipped slightly to the left before entering the second tower between floors 78 and 84 causing a shock measuring 0.7 for a duration of 6 seconds. There were 65 people on board, 9 of them crew, and the plane was flying faster than American Airlines Flight 11 (580mph). Computer simulations have show that at this speed, the aluminum wings and fuselage, together with the steel engines, traveled straight through the tower almost without slowing. The concrete floors split the plane like an ax before disintegrating into dust. Some experts claim that from that moment, the damage to the second tower was such that it should have collapsed immediately. Indeed it was the first tower to collapse, at 9:59 A.M.

"A silver flash of lightning coming from the south, a Paleolithic bird, a spear point, a scimitar glittering in the morning sunshine," Russell Banks would write in his diary. Couldn't have put it better.

9:03

ANOTHER THUNDERCLAP, ANOTHER EARTHQUAKE, ANOTHER FIREBALL.

Lourdes received an SMS from an automated news service telling her a second plane had crashed into the adjacent tower. And so it was not an accident but a terrorist attack. Who was responsible? It could be so many people. It's insane, the number of people who hate America. Including Americans. And yet I don't hate the rest of the world. I just think it's filthy, ancient, and complicated, that's all. Sheer madness . . . Jeffrey breaks down again, Anthony takes him aside. My kids are sensible, better behaved than I've ever seen them. But they can't help asking awkward questions.

"Dad, when are we gonna leave?"

"Is Mom gonna come and get us?"

"Even if it is a ride, it's way too long, isn't it?"

And so it happened: all those things I didn't understand, that I didn't want to understand; the foreign news stories I preferred to skirt, to keep out of my mind when they weren't on the TV; all these tragedies were suddenly relevant to me; these wars came to hurt me that morning; me, not someone else; my children, not someone else's; these things I knew nothing about, these events so geographically remote suddenly became the most important things in my life. I didn't want the right to intervene in the domestic affairs of foreign states, but events in the outside world had just exercised their right to interfere in mine, I didn't give a shit about wops and their homeless, drugged, raped kids with disgusting dung flies all over them, but they'd just forced their way into my house, they'd killed my fucking kids, MINE. I have to explain something: I was raised in the evangelical, Episcopalian, Methodist church of "Born Again Christians"—70 million members in the United States, including George Walker Bush, former governor of Texas, currently residing at 1600 Pennsylvania Avenue. Our credo is that Americans are the Chosen People. Europe is our Egypt, the Atlantic is our Red Sea, and America is Israel, you get the picture? Washington = Jerusalem. The Promised Land is right here. "One Nation Under God!" We don't give a shit about other people.

You didn't want them to be part of your life?

They'll be part of your death.

Lourdes collapses; she's gone to pieces. She repeats the SMS newsflash over and over: "*Breaking News: a second plane has crashed into the South Tower of the World Trade Center*"; she hands the cell phone around so all of us can read the message on the screen. Each of us reacts differently: most people let out a bewildered "Fuck!" Some sit down, take their heads in their hands. Anthony takes it out on the wall, kicking it so violently he winds up kicking a hole in it! Jeffrey cries harder, dribbling on his pink shirt. And I just crouch down, pressing my babies' heads hard against my forehead so they don't see me losing hope.

"Jerry, Dave, look, I have to come clean: this isn't a game."

"It's okay, Dad. We knew that, don't get upset."

"It's not okay, Jerry. This isn't a game, d'you get it? It's all real."

"Don't worry, we worked that out ages ago," says David, between coughing fits.

"Oh Jesus. Guys, listen to me. Maybe it's not a game, but we're gonna win anyway, together, deal?"

"But why are planes flying into the towers? Are they crazy or what?"

Looking at David's bewildered face, I can't hold back my tears any more. I become Jeffrey. I fall to my knees. I grit my teeth, I wipe my eyes, I bend, I am a curve.

"Fuck, how can people do this kind of thing to other people?"

"You shouldn't say 'fuck,' Dad."

Jerry turns away, he's ashamed to see me like this.

For more than half an hour now we've been at the top of one of the tallest skyscrapers in the world. But it's only now that I start to feel dizzy.

9:04

From Le Ciel de Paris, I gaze at the capital of France and its glorious, ancient monuments: the only thing Uncle Sam left us is our eldership. The French are so proud of their seniority, like time-serving employees calculating their pension funds. We are weighed down by the centuries. France, Egypt, England, Spain, Morocco, Holland, Portugal, Turkey, and Arabia have in their turns ruled the planet and colonized the Earth. We know all that, thanks: good riddance, it only gets you into shit. The United States, with its youthful enthusiasm, still wants to see what it feels like to be the world's boss. The old world gave up on this long ago, but the Americans are touchingly forgetful: after all, they too were colonized; they ought to remember how angry they were being occupied by a foreign power.

America hounds those they oppress into a corner, to the point where, as Brigitte Bardot purred on Serge Gainsbourg's "Bonnie & Clyde": "The only way out was death." We live in strange times; war has shifted. The battlefield is the media: in this new war Good and Evil are difficult to tell apart. Difficult to know who the good guys and the bad guys are: they change sides when we change channels. Television makes the world jealous. In the past, the poor, the colonized, didn't spend their nights in their shanty towns staring at wealth on a screen. They didn't realize that some countries had everything while they slogged their guts out for nothing. In France, the Revolution would have happened a lot earlier if the serfs had had a little screen where they could see the opulence of kings and queens. Nowadays, all over the world, the dirty countries hover between awe and contempt, fascination and disgust for the clean countries whose lifestyles they pick up on satellite with their hacked decoders using a sieve for a satellite dish. It is a recent phenomenon: we call it globalization, but its real name is television. Economics, broadcasting, cinema, marketing are all globalized, but the rest—the politics and the social issues—doesn't follow.

OK, I'll stop there, not being competent to analyze everything. If you want to unravel the geopolitical tangle of terrorism, call the offices of Spengler, Huntington, Baudrillard, Adler, Fukuyama, Revel . . . But I can't guarantee that things will immediately become clearer.

The view this morning is magnificent. The view depends on the day. This morning at 9:04 A.M., the Eiffel Tower glitters on my right, the steel edifice built by the same Gustave who buttressed the Statue of Liberty. To the right, Les Invalides, where Napoleon Bonaparte is laid, the man who sold Louisiana to the Americans for 15 million dollars (say what you like: the Emperor was a better businessman than the Algonquin Indians who handed over Manhattan to Peter Minuit, a French-born Huguenot, for 24 bucks). Between them, the Arc de Triomphe on the Place de l'Étoile, far off in the white, Triumph off in the distance. All those stone blocks so fragile . . . I did what I promised myself: I went down the stairs. Fifty-six floors. My first impression was the monotony, then dizziness. Then, rapidly, fear and claustrophobia mount. Alone in that stairwell, I tried to imagine what the passing minutes were like for the hundreds descending. Almost all of those who worked on the floors below the point at which the plane entered the building emerged unscathed. They didn't panic because they did not know what I know now. They had faith in the solidity of buildings. They took their time. They followed the orders of firefighters who would die in the minutes that followed. They left calmly, and then, as they turned, they saw this solid building disintegrate into a pile of rubble.

The good thing about going back down Tour Montparnasse without your daughter is that rue de la Gaieté is nearby. So you can walk around the sex shops, the theaters, the Japanese restaurants. The embarrassing thing is if someone recognizes me and asks me for an autograph as I'm walking out of a peep show. It's embarrassing shaking hands with someone when I've just wiped my own with a Kleenex. It's stupid but I can't help blushing: fucking Catholicism is still part of me.

Walking up the Boulevard Edgar-Quinet, I pass a hostess bar (Le Monocle Elle et Lui: strange name), a famous swingers' club (the 2+2), and several funeral parlors. After that, I follow the walls of Montparnasse Cemetery where Sartre, de Beauvoir, Duras, Cioran, Beckett, and Ionesco are buried . . . Montparnasse is a neighborhood of sex, literature, and death; this is probably the reason Americans like it so much. I go into the cemetery and head toward the grave of Charles Baudelaire, a former pupil of the Lycée Louis-le-Grand. DEAD AT 46. His small white grave is a pitiful sight next to the mausoleum of his neighbor, the illustrious Charles Sapey, SENATOR, HIGH-RANKING OFFICER OF THE LEGION OF HONOR, FORMER DEPUTY FOR THE CONSTITUENCY OF ISÈRE, DIED MAY 5 1857. The poet lies with his father-in-law, General Aupick, and his twice-widowed mother. On the far side of the cemetery, a strange monument has been erected in Baudelaire's honor: it consists of the recumbent beribboned effigy of the artist, like an Egyptian mummy upon which the "*génie du mal*" is perched sculpted in stone, leaning on a balustrade like Rodin's "Thinker." Stooped, disagreeable, with his huge biceps, the "genius of evil" sits enthroned facing the Tour Montparnasse, seeming to scorn it with his prominent chin. I take out my Polaroid.

The Genius of Evil . . .

. . . and what he surveys

I leave the cemetery and walk back up the boulevard to the Cartier foundation, where there is a huge exhibition of accidents staged by Paul Virilio. I walk down the concrete steps (more steps!) and arrive in a basement filled with dull mechanical rumblings.

9:05

IN THE ROOF SPACE ON THE 109TH FLOOR, THE ATTIC OF THE World, through the wall of smoke, I watch the crowd streaming away from us. I give the kids a leg up to get to the meager fresh air. It's a desperate flight for the air. If I'd known, I would have brought oxygen tanks, or gas masks. In any case, soon everyone in the West will walk round with gas masks slung over their shoulders.

Anthony is back with a bleary Jeffrey. He got him to take a couple of Xanax. He looks strange, like a deflated punching bag. Anthony looks even more miserable than Jeffrey. Lourdes quietly breaks down and cries. I take her hand, stroking it like I used to stroke a kitten I once had. Little by little, the masks, and the people, fall away. The heat is getting closer. Fear like a viral infection sets up house in us. I have only to see the despair in Jeffrey's eyes to be infected. I hold back, determined not to look at my sons so that they don't see the resignation in my eyes. Nobody must suspect that I'm giving up hope. We're sitting on the floor in front of the only exit: a thick, red, steel-plated fire door on which is written the words EMERGENCY EXIT. Around us, the moaning is unrelenting. Groups of haggard people arrive, reeling like incredulous zombies. Hope is the most painful thing in the world. I could not bear another disappointment.

Fucking hell, what would Bruce Willis do in my shoes? Jeffrey's phone manages to get a signal: he calls his boyfriend. I can hear his partner sobbing from here. Jeffrey's gay, but he wears a wedding ring. Marriage is such bullshit. For God's sake, I can't let emotion get the better of me. I've got to be brave in front of the kids. Jerry's nosebleed has stopped, so that's something at least. I'm losing it, this kind of barbarism has me eaten up with hate. How could they do this to us? I grew up during the Cold War; it was all so simple back then. . . . America only had one enemy: Russia. It was useful, having one, fuck-off, clear-cut enemy; it gave everyone else a choice. Do you want your supermarkets full or empty? Do you want the right to criticize or the duty to shut the fuck up? Nowadays, with nothing to counterbalance it, America has become the Goliath to be slain. America has become its own worst enemy.

I don't know what makes me think of Genesis. Maybe I'm remembering something from Sunday school: the Methodists consult the first book of the Bible a lot; some "creationist" lunatics still reject Darwinism. My parents' puritanical Calvinism was based almost entirely on the Old Testament. According to them, Adam and Eve really existed, not to mention the apple, the serpent, Cain and Abel, the flood, Noah's ark, etc. . . . And the Tower of Babel? I wonder if that's where I am now. You know the story: it appears in several Mesopotamian writings: men learn to make tools and decide to build a tower to reach the heavens. They want to "make a name for themselves lest they be scattered abroad upon the face of the whole earth." God does not approve of their decision: man must not be prideful, man must not take himself for God. You might have thought that, to punish him, God would destroy the tower in a furious rage, but not at all. The word Babel represents Babylon, but brings language to mind (hence the verb "to babble"). God avenges himself in a much more cruel and twisted fashion, by preventing men from using the same words to denote objects. God decides to create chaos in language on earth. God chooses to dissolve language: hereafter, things will be known by many different names, the link between word and object will be lost; for presuming to build this tower, men will cease to understand one another. Divine punishment takes the form of preventing men from communicating with one another. The Tower of Babel was the first attempt at globalization. If, as millions of Americans do, we take Genesis absolutely literally, then God is opposed to globalization. The Judeo-Christian faith is founded on the idea that there must be simultaneous interpreters, languages which are foreign to each other, that there must be bread on the table before one can pass on the Scriptures, that the human race is divided into exotic idioms and uncertain babble. God has set his face against New York.

Genesis 11:5–8

And the LORD came down to see the city and the tower, which the children of men builded. And the LORD said, Behold, the people is one, and they have all one language; and this they begin to do: and now nothing will be restrained for them, which they have imagined to do. Go to, let us go down, and there confound their language, that they may not understand one another's speech. So the LORD scattered them abroad from thence upon the face of the earth, and they left off to build the city.

9:06

At 9:06 a.m., Glen Vogt, general manager of Windows on the World, was (fortunately for him) not at his place of work. Twenty minutes after the plane entered the building, his assistant, Christine Olender, called him at home. She got his wife instead, because he was on the street by the World Trade Center getting a crick in his neck, shocked by the disaster. Ms. Olender told Mrs. Vogt that they hadn't heard anything about how to leave. "The ceilings are falling," she said. "The floors are buckling," she added. At least 41 people in the restaurant succeeded in getting a call through to someone outside the building.

That morning, three torches burned in New Amsterdam: the torch atop the Statue of Liberty, that of the North Tower, that of the South Tower.

There is another eyewitness account from Windows on the World: that of Ivhan Luyis Carpio, in a call to his cousin. "I can't go anywhere because they told us not to move. I have to wait for the firefighters." It is plausible that a high percentage of the restaurant's customers meekly obeyed the order to stay put, while struggling to get air, smashing the windows, climbing on tables to avoid being burned. But we also have evidence of numerous calls to 911 from the roof, which seems to indicate that some of the customers disobeyed to escape to the fresh air.

Can a human being melt?

Someone else summed up the situation very clearly: "We're trapped," Howard Kane said to his wife Laurie.

What no one said: everyone was vomiting.

Even if I go deep, deep into the horror, my book will always remain 1,350 feet below the truth.

9:07

"We've got a problem."

Anthony keeps trying his cell phone. Anthony's got a problem. Something that's been bothering him for a while back that he hasn't dared tell us. Something that leaves a fathomless sadness deep in his eyes.

"What? What's the problem?"

"My key won't open the door on its own. Someone downstairs at the security desk has to push a button. And I can't get through to them. I can't get a signal on the cell phone and the internal phones are cut off—"

"Spare me the bullshit! [I could also have said "Cut the crap," but that would be less refined.] Where are they, these security guards?"

"The control center is on the 22nd floor, but they're not answering. Jesus, if the control center has been evacuated, there's nothing I can do. They have to release the lock with the buzzer. If they don't we're stuck. And that doesn't make me any happier than it does you guys."

Jeffrey comes out of his torpor:

"Never mind the fucking buzzer! We'll break the fucking door down!"

Anthony would like to share his optimism.

"The door's secured. We couldn't even open it with a power drill. And we haven't got a power drill."

"FUCKING SHIT! HOW THE FUCK ARE WE GONNA GET OUT OF HERE?"

Jeffrey has picked up a machine, a huge, heavy, cast-iron thing, and is using it to pound the lock. He works furiously, hammering at it with all his strength. Anthony and I step back so we don't get our heads caved in by this thing he's swinging with those muscular arms he's got from working out regularly in some gym in the East Village.

Anthony shakes his head. I realize that I hate this man, that I admire Jeffrey all the more. His co-workers are counting on him, and he's determined not to let them down. Fatalism sickens me. I much prefer the energy of despair, the ferocity of nature, the instinct to survive. I'm not prepared to admit defeat until I've dislocated both my shoulders on this door. I want to sweat, to try anything, to go on believing. Under Jeffrey's bludgeoning, the door handle gives way, but the door remains tightly sealed. He turns to us, looking helpless, but his despair inspires only respect. I hope that Jerry and David haven't heard any of this. They're standing on the ledge of a fanlight with Lourdes. They're not scared of heights anymore now that they're suffocating. Jerry's napkin is stained with blood, like his T-shirt. "It looks bad, but it's not serious; he gets nosebleeds all the time." I say it over and over trying to convince myself.

* * *

Anthony huddles over his cell phone, obstinately pressing the green redial button. He has to get through to the security staff, or failing that, the cops. I can hear police helicopters on the other side of the door. I refuse to burn to death just because some emergency exit is stopping them from rescuing us. Nine-One-One. Nine-One-One. S.O.S. S.O.S. Just like the end of *Johnny Got His Gun*. Save our souls.

I go back to join the boys to get a breath of air from outside. Perched on Lourdes's shoulders, they repeat the prayers she's saying aloud. In the past, they used to put gargoyles at the top of buildings to protect them, like on the Chrysler Building. Sculptures made to look like dragons, monsters, demons like the ones at the top of the towers of Notre Dame de Paris, intended to drive away devils and ward off invaders. Will my children, these little blond gargoyles leaning into the void, be enough to ward off evil spirits? Why did architects stop treating skyscrapers as cathedrals? If they put gargoyles at the top of towers there must have been a reason. Why would they do so, if not . . . in anticipation of what has just happened to us? They knew that one day danger would come from the air. In those moments of terror, prayer comes to us unbidden. Religion is reborn in us. In the minutes ahead of us, the World Trade Center, a temple to atheism and to international lucre, will gradually become a makeshift church.

9:08

IN *THE JOKE* BY MILAN KUNDERA, ONE OF THE CHARACTERS ASKS the question: "Do you think destructions can be beautiful?" I move about like a sleepwalker, stunned by the exhibition "*Ce qui arrive*" mounted by philosopher and urban planner Paul Virilio in collaboration with Agence France Presse and the Institut National de l'Audiovisuel from November 29, 2002, to March 30, 2003. On the walls of the Fondation Cartier hang sepia photographs of a train wreck that took place at the Gare Montparnasse on October 22, 1895: a steam locomotive piled straight through the second floor facade before falling onto the cobbles of the square outside. A crowd of men in derbies surrounds the mangled wreck. The exhibition consists of a succession of dark, noisy rooms in which videos of disasters are being projected. Everywhere there is smoke and security guards communicating on walkie-talkies. Images of the diggers at Ground Zero appear on a giant screen (a looped ten-minute digital video by Tony Oursler): an immense column of white smoke overshadows a colossal heap of scrap iron; a few minuscule human beings wander around the cranes, which resemble helpless grasshoppers. In the background, a number of prefabricated concrete sections of the World Trade Center still stand, forming a pitiful rampart. What is most striking is the mud. This edifice of concrete and steel has been transformed into a muddy heap. Man-made purity has given way to natural filth. The smooth, glittering towers have been reduced to a hideous, chaotic mess. Now I understand what the sculptor César intended by crushing cars. The bulldozers would try to tidy up this mess, to rediscover the purity of glass, the perfection of the past. It's impossible not to feel a lump in your throat considering such carnage. Nonetheless, I can't shake a feeling of disquiet, the very feeling I have writing this book: does one have the right? Is it normal to be quite so fascinated with destruction? Kundera's question resonates oddly among these disasters. The New York streets are white with paper and dust as if it had been snowing; in the middle of the image, a black baby sleeps in a stroller. Virilio's exhibition caused a scandal when it opened. Isn't it too early to make art of such misery? Of course, art is not obligatory and no one is obliged to visit an exhibition or read a book. All the same, "*Ce qui arrive*" collects disasters as one might collect trophies: images of mercury pollution in Minamata, Japan, 1973; a dioxin leak at the Icmesa factory, Seveso, Italy, 1976; a plane crash in Tenerife, Spain, 1977; the wreck of the oil tanker *Amoco Cadiz*, Finistère, France, 1978. Some of the spectators wipe their eyes, blow their noses, turn away, refuse to confront the images. I know how they feel. And yet this is our world and for the moment we cannot live anywhere else. Radioactive gas leak, Three Mile Island, Pennsylvania, 1979; toxic gas leak, Union Carbide plant, Bhopal, India, 1979. Explosion of the space shuttle *Challenger*, Cape Canaveral, Florida, 1986. Virilio's perspective can be seen as shocking: merging industrial accidents with terrorist attacks. Nuclear reactor meltdown at Chernobyl nuclear facility, Ukraine, 1986. Wreck of the *Exxon Valdez*, Alaska, 1989. Sarin gas attack, Tokyo subway, Japan, 1995. To these he adds natural disasters like the hurricane in France in 1999, the bushfires in Australia in 1997, the earthquake in Kobe, Japan, 1995. All underscored by a soundtrack of dramatic film music. I stroll among these monstrosities. I would gladly wash my hands of them, I'd like to think that I am not complicit in such horrors. And yet, like every human being, at a microscopic level, I am complicit. Freud's quotation is emblazoned above the entrance: "Accumulation puts an end to the impression of chance." This enigmatic sentence, which dates from 1914–1915, seems to answer David's question earlier:

"What's a coindesense?"

The greater the scientific progress, the more violent the accidents, the more beautiful the destruction. At the conclusion of the exhibition, Virilio unquestionably takes provocation too far, screening a TV broadcast of an astonishing fireworks display over Shanghai: he dares to establish a link between unadulterated horror and aesthetic beauty. The exhibition left a nasty taste in my mouth. I left feeling even more guilty than before. Can the destruction of the Twin Towers really be presented side by side with a fireworks display, be it the most grandiose in the world? Oh, the beautiful flames, oh, the beautiful blue, oh the beautiful burning bodies? Will I be able to look myself in the eye after publishing this book? It makes me feel like throwing up my Ciel de Paris breakfast, but I'm forced to admit that my eye develops a taste for the horrific. I love the vast column of smoke pouring from the towers on the giant screen, projected in real time, the white plume against the blue of the sky, like a silk scarf hanging suspended between land and sea. I love it, not only because of its ethereal splendor, but because I know the apocalypse it portends, the violence and the horror it contains. Virilio forces me to face that part of my humanity that is not humanist.

9:09

Dad's cure for when he's scared is to just keep talking.

"Soon as they airlift us out of here, I'm taking you guys to FAO Schwarz and you can have anything you want. A big splurge."

"Can I get a Dr Pepper?"

"Sure. You know your great-great-grandfather nearly put money in the Coca-Cola Company? Did I ever tell you this story? Back then, the family lived in Atlanta. One day, this little druggist who lived in town came by: he was looking for money to launch a new tonic that he'd just perfected. Since we were one of the wealthy patrician families in town, he naturally asked your great-great-grandfather if he wanted to share in the profits. The story become a standing joke in the Yorston family: the little druggist was invited to dinner at the mansion. He gave the whole family this weird concoction made of coca leaves to taste. Everyone thought it was disgusting, undrinkable. 'Besides, the color is repulsive!' 'Ugh! It'll never sell!' The druggist defended his potion, explaining that it contained vitamins and aided digestion. Your ancestor burst out laughing and hollered 'This sure is the first time I've been asked to invest in a laxative.' And the inventor of Coca-Cola left without a cent. For years the family laughed about it, then one day, they stopped laughing: if we'd helped out that little druggist, we'd be in the *Forbes* Top 100 today."

Dad's told this story, like, thirty times, but I never get tired of it. He looks so happy when Jerry and me listen to his stories. I like the idea we were almost rich. Every time I drink a can of Coke I think how I could have been Mister Big. No point getting pissed at the old guys. I read about this stuff in class. They had, like, plantations full of slaves that picked the cotton. How were they supposed to know they'd be wiped out by the war with the Yankees. Anyway, later on, they struck oil. Actually, they were a bunch of dumb rednecks, sometimes they just got lucky, sometimes not. A bit like today. Like, first, everything's cool, we're cutting class, we get to go to New York, the pancakes are wicked, Dad lets us mess around pressing the buttons in the elevator, making them light up and go "ding," it was dope. But now, with the fire and all, everything stinks, Jerry's got a nosebleed, and I'm coughing all the time, it's a bit heavy. Lourdes is really nice with us, but she cries nonstop, it's a real bummer. Anthony's cool, Jeffrey's, like, completely out of it, forever going off to check on his group and coming back to see if he can get a signal on the cell phone. They're good people, but the whole thing is skank. Dad has to use his secret superpowers, the ones that only appear when there's megadanger. He'll probably mutate in a couple of nanoseconds: it's like Clark Kent, you have to give him time to get into his gear. Like, right now, all he wants to do is talk about grandparents passing up the deal of the century and stuff, but nobody cares. Jeez, I hate it when this happens in comics—you have to wait, like, forever before the hero gets around to saving the people trapped in the burning building. It's boring, but that's always how it happens. If the hero showed up right at the start, there wouldn't be any suspense. Same thing with *Dragonball* on TV. The guys who make cartoons are smart: they know you have to make the kids wait around. So we wait. That's all kids ever get to do anyway. Wait till we grow up before we can pig out on M&Ms and go to Universal Studios all the time without having to beg the 'rents. To kill time, I make out like I'm really interested in Dad's story.

"Is that really true, Dad? Really? We were nearly the Coca-Cola family."

And Dad's, like, all happy and he's stopped crying and stuff, it's really cool seeing him smile, "It's true, David—can you imagine?," and Jerry's like "What?" because he knows the story by heart, and he can't figure out why I'm faking like this is the first time I heard it. Like, duh! I'm doing it to keep Dad happy, otherwise he's not gonna have enough energy to use his superpowers.

9:10

La Closerie des Lilas (1804), Le Dôme (1897), La Rotonde (1911), Le Sélect (1925), La Coupole (1927). The Lost Generation knew where to find each other: Montparnasse. In pilgrimage, I stagger thorough the bars Hemingway catalogs in *A Moveable Feast*: thanks to "Papa," writing is the perfect excuse for getting drunk on your own, especially if you've just had a bust-up with your girlfriend. When I order a vermouth-cassis at the Closerie, it's purely professional courtesy. What on earth were these geniuses thinking, drinking an abomination like this? I pass 27 rue de Fleurus, a couple of minutes from my house, where Gertrude Stein and Alice Babette Toklas lived. To my stupefaction, a plaque reminds us of the importance of this mythical apartment where Gauguins and Mirós hung on the walls and where the famous line "You are all a lost generation" was uttered by Ms. Stein's car mechanic as he leaned over her creaky old Model T with the iffy transmission. Gertrude Stein, the American who introduced Picasso to Matisse, had been living in Paris since 1902, in a ground floor apartment with a courtyard garden. It's a neighborhood in which the Russians preceded the Americans. Hemingway came here on the advice of Sherwood Anderson and tried to be like Modigliani, Soutine, Chagall, etc. Trotsky and Lenin planned the revolution here. Why, when he was about to put a bullet in his head, did Hemingway come back here in spirit? In 1957, when he begins writing *A Moveable Feast,* he is fifty-eight. Three years earlier, he received the Nobel Prize for Literature. Four years later, he will kill himself with a hunting rifle. He decides to spend those last four years in the time machine we call literature. Physically he is in Ketchum (Idaho), then Spain and later Cuba. But in his mind, the last years of his life take place in the Paris of 1921–1926, with his first wife, Hadley Richardson. He refuses to be sixty: he writes so that he can be twenty-five again, so he can once again be the young unknown, destitute but in love, who first met Scott Fitzgerald in April 1925, blind drunk in the Dingo Bar on rue Delambre (now L'Auberge de Venise), where seventy-eight years later I scribble these words, drinking a Long Island Ice Tea (which recipe he invented: all the white spirits in a tumbler plus Coca Cola and ice). At the Dingo Bar, you could run into Isadora Duncan, Tristan Tzara (who is buried in Montparnasse Cemetery), Man Ray. . . . I raise my glass to the great artists who haunt these wood-paneled walls perfumed with cigar smoke, bourbon, and despair.

It was not by accident that Pompidou built the miniature replica of the World Trade Center in Montparnasse: this was a district whose soul had been imported from America. Hemingway wanted to retrace his steps; I am doing it on his behalf. At 42 rue du Montparnasse, the Falstaff is still there, but the brothel on the corner has disappeared: Le Sphinx, 31 Boulevard Edgar-Quinet, with its Egyptian suite, where Henry Miller spent money he didn't have. Nowadays, it's a branch of the Banque

Populaire, with an ATM out front. Walking home (with difficulty), I look for 113 rue Notre-Dame-des-Champs, where Hemingway settled himself in 1924 when he got back from Toronto (Ezra Pound lived on the same street at 70 *bis*). I pass 115, then 111. Hey, number 113 has disappeared too, though it wasn't a whorehouse. I retrace my steps . . . I'm not imagining it: rue Notre-Dame-des-Champs skips from 111 to 115—you can go and check for yourself. So the building where F. Scott Fitzgerald pissed on the stairs, starting a memorable row between Ernest Hemingway and his concierge, no longer exists. All that remains of it is a book: *A Moveable Edifice.* There isn't even a plaque. Pity, there's quite a lot you could chisel into the marble. "Here the American writer Ernest Hemingway loved his wife Hadley and his son Bumby, where he was visited by Gertrude Stein, Sylvia Beach, William Carlos Williams, John Dos Passos, where he wrote *The Sun Also Rises*, where F. Scott Fitzgerald urinated in the doorway one Saturday night in 1925 angering the concierge, where Hemingway received a letter of apology from Fitzgerald in which he said: 'The deplorable man who entered your apartment Saturday morning was not me but a man named Johnston has often been mistaken for me.'"

The moral of the story is: when buildings vanish, only books can remember them. This is why Hemingway wrote about Paris before he died. Because he knew that books are more durable than buildings.

9:11

Ultra-secret communication from secret agent David Yorston to the Forces of the Galactic Alliance

SEPTEMBER 11, 2001. I HAVE DISCOVERED MY FATHER POSSESSES superpowers. I was with my older brother in Windows on the World when it happened. Officially, my father is called Carthew, but that's not his real name. He didn't know he had mega-extrasensory powers, like in *X-Men* when the guy realizes he can see through walls when he didn't even know himself. I knew because I had been informed by the Intergalactic Charter in 7987 BN (Before Now) (I'm an agent of the Intergalactic Council). In fact, my father's name is not Carthew, it's Ultra-Dude. We don't know the extent of his powers, because he hasn't used them yet, since they operate only when he is in megadanger, like in a fire for instance. At times like this, he can walk through concrete walls, twist metal, even fly, since fear charges his battery-pack. Then afterward, he doesn't remember anything because he's got an instantaneous auto-adaptive memory that allows him to erase all the data from his mental hard drive so he doesn't give up the microfilm if he's ever subjected to cunning interrogations in an Astral Confederation prison ruled by his arch enemy Morg (aka Jerry the Vile).

I was eating pancakes with a number of Earthlings when we were attacked by the Dark Forces: it was a carefully planned attack, most likely an attempt by Lieutenant Devil-Raptor to take Ultra-Dude by surprise. Using the secret transformer concealed beneath the North Pole for thousands of years, the evil Devil-Raptor transformed himself into a plane and, using teleportation, slammed into the skyscraper trying to get at the macro-constrictive primes (Devil-Raptor is an interstellar prime hunter capable of subliminal transformations: he can transform himself into anything he touches, except if he's got a flu). Anyway, the attack happened just a few minutes ago. I will make contact again to keep you informed of developments. In a moment, as soon as he senses his devastating googolplex superpowers, Ultra-Dude will take action. For the moment, he is completely unaware that he is a superhero about to avenge the abomination of Darkness and also the ghastly murder of his mother, who was gobbled up by the Hideous Fang Fish twelve centuries ago. Ultra-Dude will wake in a second, and there's gonna be megadeath. They'll see! Devil-Raptor will get what's coming to him when Ultra-Dude zaps him with his dematerializing Starlaser. The battle has only just started. With the help of the Ark of the Covenant and the Sacred Ring, Ultra-Dude will take on the puny enemy minions with his Magic Fire. Agent X275 signing off.

9:12

"LES PLANTES SONT PLUS AWARE QUE LES AUTRES SPECIES"; "Manger des cacahuètes, it's a really strong feeling." I like *Franglais*; it's the language of the future. A book celebrating it has just been published: an anthology of quotations by Hollywood-based Belgian kickboxer cum actor, Jean-Claude Van Damme. "La drogue c'est comme quand tu close your eyes"; "Un biscuit ça n'a pas de spirit." In 2050, everyone will speakera like Jean-Claude Van Damme, hero of *Replicant*. "Mourir, c'est vraiment strong." "Personne n'est right or wrong." Young people holed up in their audiovisual loft spaces have taken up the adroit path of the Belgian cyborg quite spontaneously: "Je suis pas très free du body." "Moi je dis yes à la life." "Est-ce que tu kiffes la night?" "Je navigue au feeling." We shouldn't be afraid of English words. They are calmly integrated into our own in order to create a global language, one that defies God: the single language of Babel. Les words du world. The lexicon of text messaging ("CU L8R"), Internet emoticons (:-)), the rise of phonetic spelling and slang, all of this contributes to creating the novspeak of the third millennium. Anyway, whatever. Let's leave the last word to Jean-Claude Van Damme: "A single language, a single currency and no religion and everyone would be better off. But we're not here to talk politics."

I also love lots of disgusting American things like Vanilla Coke, peanut butter, cheesecake, onion rings, garlic butter, chicken wings, root beer.

Above all, I love Hugh Hefner, founder of *Playboy*. Our fathers all wanted to be like him. It's important to understand what happened to our parents' generation in the sixties with every filthy rich guy thinking he was Hugh Hefner. His vast orgy-filled mansion, his private jet, transformed twentieth-century masculinity. To be a modern man in the sixties was to be a womanizer. The new Don Juan had to drive a fast car, smoke American cigarettes, sit around turquoise swimming pools surrounded by big-breasted blondes in bikinis. Nowadays, that type of masculinity has become obsolete. There's nothing sleazier than a playboy in a nightclub; in fact, that desperate attempt at seduction is precisely what marks a man out as old, no matter how many facelifts he's had. Mademoiselle, if a guy with graying temples and a playboy shtick hits on you, he must be at least seventy, since he's stuck in the thirty-five-year-old time warp from the year he turned thirty-five.

In the America of the sixties and seventies, the playboy was a superman. Any self-respecting man had to come on like Tom Jones, Gunter Sachs, Porfirio Rubirosa, Malko Linge, Julio Iglesias, Kurt Jürgens, Roger Moore, Roger Vadim, Warren Beatty, Burt Reynolds. You had to wear your shirt open with a lot of chest hair peeking out. You had to pick up a different girl every night at all costs. You had to be tanned all year round. Everything that today, in the 00s, is the height of the passé, the pathetic, was an absolute must. In France, Eddie Barclay and Sasha Distel, Jean-Paul Belmondo and Philippe Junot were the true icons of the middle classes, much more than hippies and rock stars. Add to this the arrival of the contraceptive pill, relaxed divorce laws, the feminist revolution, the sexual revolution and you get the INTERNATIONAL PLAYBOY: "the man without seriousness" described by psychiatrist Charles Melman, the man who must "have pleasure at any price." What had happened? Freedom had killed off marriage and the family, couples and children. Faithfulness had become a concept that was reactionary, impossible, inhuman. In this new world, love was a three-year thing, max. Nowadays, the INTERNATIONAL PLAYBOY lives on. He lurks within each of us; he has been inexorably absorbed by every man. The INTERNATIONAL PLAYBOY is single because he refuses to be tied down. He changes nationality every other week. He lives alone and dies alone. He has no friends, only a few urbane, professional acquaintances. He speaks *Franglais*. When he goes out, it's to hunt bimbos (in French, "*pétasse*"). In the early days, when he is rich and handsome, he seduces shallow women. Later, when he is not as rich and not as handsome, he will pay prostitutes to escort him. He never looks for love, only for pleasure. He loves no one, especially not himself, because he refuses to suffer and does not want to risk losing face. The INTERNATIONAL PLAYBOY takes his champagne showers in Saint-Tropez, hits on venal women in hotel bars, winds up in swingers' clubs with some rented creature. Of course, he's kitsch (in France, Jean-Pierre Marielle has often parodied him; in the United States, Mike Myers did so in *Austin Powers*) but he paves the way for twenty-first-century mutant man: doped up on Viagra until he drops dead. His embarrassing behavior, his sockless feet in his moccasins to stay young, the INTERNATIONAL PLAYBOY poses serious questions: what use is love in a civilization based on desire? Why burden yourself with a family if freedom is the ultimate principle? What is the purpose of morality in a hedonistic society? If God is dead, then the whole world is a brothel, and the only thing to do is make the most of it until you buy the farm. If the individual is king, then only selfishness makes sense. And if the father is no longer the sole figure of authority, then the only thing that limits violence in a materialistic democracy is the police.

9:13

The only thing standing between me and greatness is me.

—Woody Allen

BELOW US: GLASS DOORS, PLANTS, COLONNADES, POLISHED PARquet floors, lamps with white lampshades of extraordinary sophistication . . . polished wooden balustrades, fawn leather benches, an ocher bar . . .

Above us: Helicopters whirling like aluminum hornets, a column of smoke extending the tower to 2,000 feet.

Us: Trembling humans huddled around a locked door surrounded by machines, pipes, deafened by the noise of the supercharged pumps and the hydraulic generators.

I look at Jerry. From this angle, he looks a lot like me. Lucky for David, he looks less like me. But I clearly reproduced; it's undeniable. And then got the hell out of there in a hurry. If society offers you the choice of listening to a baby screaming or going to a party without your wife, it's hardly surprising that there are more and more single mothers in the West. I know exactly what Jerry thinks of me because he told me. He thinks I'm James Bond: the sort of guy who sleeps with every girl he meets.

David, on the other hand, thinks I'm some sort of superhero:

"Hey, Dad, you know you don't have to keep hiding your superpowers."

The advantage of hitting on different girls all the time is that you can always use the same lines. It's very relaxing.

Jeffrey shows me a bottle of 1929 Haut-Brion.

"Hey, we might as well drink it. I found a case of the stuff in the corridor. I don't see why we should deprive ourselves. I gave the rest of the bottles to my group!"

"Careful not to mix it with the pills . . ."

"What the hell! Come on! Enjoy!"

Jeffrey uncorks the *grand cru français* and chugalugs straight from the bottle.

"Wow. It needs time to breathe, but it's nectar . . ."

"I think we all need time to breathe," says Anthony. "Where'd you get that bottle?"

"Relax, I'm just borrowing it, the company will pick up the tab. Don't worry, be happy . . ."

I drink from the bottle. The antique purple liquor, which dates from the crash of '29, trickles down my throat like a last caress, a devil's kiss. It would be wrong to refuse; it's comforting. I proffer the bottle to Anthony, who shakes his head.

"No thanks. I don't do alcohol, I'm a practicing Muslim."

"Fuck! And I'm Jewish!" shouts Jeffrey, grabbing the bottle of Haut-Brion and pouring the wine into his open mouth. "So you're trying to kill all of us. You happy with what your buddies have done here?"

"Come on! We don't know who did this. It could have been anybody."

"Aw, come off it, suicide bombers is your thing. You blow yourself up in some pizza joint and Allah rewards you."

Anthony gets angry.

"Fuck, I'm a Muslim, not a fanatic, gimme a break, man."

"Take it easy, Tony," I say, grabbing the bottle from Jeffrey. "He's been mixing alcohol and tranquilizers. He's losing it, that's all."

"Yeah, I'm losing it all right," says Jeffrey. "I must be losing it 'cos I'm just some faggot, right? Like, I'm the one crashing planes into buildings and butchering innocent people just to wipe out the state of Israel?"

Oh shit. I take another big swig of 1929 Haut-Brion before wading in as Boutros Boutros.

"Look, I'm Christian, he's Muslim, you're Jewish, which means we all believe in the same God, OK? Now calm down. Best thing we can do is pray in our three religions, that way God's three times more likely to listen and open this fucking door!"

Wine is the answer to religious conflict. Anthony should try some. He sits down again and starts punching numbers into his cell phone. Jeffrey chugs the wine and chuckles: "It's not even kosher!"

Jerry laughs, so do I. David's still daydreaming. Lourdes is still leaning out the window. I'd like to tell you a bunch of crazy action-packed anecdotes full of twists and surprises, but the truth is: nothing happened. We waited for someone to come for us and nobody came. It smelled of burning carpet and the Mars bars melting in the vending machines down below in the belly of the beast.

9:14

I'M REALLY PISSED AT THE GUY WHO INVENTED THE OFFICE PARAchute for not inventing it until after the tragedy. It's not as though it's complicated: couldn't you have thought of it sooner, asshole? I would have loved to see hundreds of men and women hurling themselves into space, backpacks on, parachutes unfurling over the WTC plaza. I would have liked to see them glide through the air, defying gravity and terrorists, set down on the concrete, fall into the arms of the firefighters.

Same goes for the architects who decided to stop putting external fire escapes on buildings. There's one on every building in New York, except those with too many floors: in other words, the very buildings that need them most. It would look ugly on a skyscraper? Beware: design kills. Was a 110-story external staircase so inconceivable?

And why hasn't airline security changed? Security staff still cast a vague glance as your bags go through the X-ray machine. Sometimes they rummage through a piece of luggage on a hunch.

On planes, they've replaced metal knives with plastic. But they still have metal forks! Like you couldn't kill someone with a fork. Just aim for the eyes or the throat. Haven't they seen Joe Pesci in *Casino*?

Why aren't there security guards on every plane? They've got them outside every nightclub! Are nightclubs so much more dangerous than planes? At the moment, passenger safety is left in the hands of air hostesses with easily pierced throats.

It would also have been possible to throw ropes to the victims, which they could have used to escape, like crooks tying sheets to the bars of their cells to slide down the walls. Why didn't they try something like that? Or rope ladders thrown towards the side that wasn't burning. Or organize huge inflatable air beds like in *Lethal Weapon* to break the jumpers' fall.

The fact is, nobody believed the towers could collapse. Too much faith in technology. Singular lack of imagination. Confidence in the supremacy of reality over fiction.

"It's like being inside a chimney," says one of the firefighters in Irwin Allen and John Guillermin's *The Towering Inferno* (released in 1974, the year the World Trade Center was inaugurated). The fact that they didn't attempt an air rescue is probably because the cops had seen the movie in which police drop cables from a helicopter in an attempt to save people trapped by a fire on the top floor of a skyscraper. In the film, the chopper crashes onto the roof. At 9:14, the police probably didn't want life to imitate art.

9:15

FOR HALF AN HOUR NOW WE'VE HAD A PLANE UNDER OUR FEET

Still no evacuation

We are metal shrieking

People hanging out the windows

People falling from the windows

An abandoned wheelchair

Brokers' offices but no brokers

A stapler forgotten on a photocopier

Filing cabinets overturned with the files still filed

A diary full of urgent appointments

A weather forecast predicting clear skies and a high of 79°F this morning

All the windows blown out

Blazing fuel in the elevator shafts

98 elevators, all out of order

White marble in the open spaces stained with blood

Two corridors lit with small halogens like dotted lines in the ceiling

Ocher flames with blue curls of smoke

Scraps of paper dancing in the air like the Fourth of July

The trash of the peoples of the whole world

United Colors of Babel

Hands in tatters
skin hanging from arms
like an Issey Miyake dress

Pretty women weeping
Pieces of fuselage on the escalators
Pretty women coughing

No contact with the outside world
Plates and cups, white and blue, in pieces
Everything is hazy dusty dead filthy
Silence pierced by alarms

Carved-up faces by the coffee machine

A closed space with a fire down below
We roast
We are being roasted like chickens

Smoked like salmon
Alarms full tilt

Dust in the wind
All we are is
Dust in the wind

In the heat, the figurative paintings melt
And become abstracts

A rain of bodies over the WTC Plaza.

9:16

I'VE OFTEN THOUGHT ABOUT WHAT MAKES PEOPLE JUMP IN A FIRE. It's because they know they're going to die. They have no more air, they're suffocating, they're burning. If they're going to die, they might as well die quickly and cleanly. "Jumpers" are not depressed, they're rational people. They've weighed the pros and the cons and prefer the dizzying freefall to being burned alive. They choose the swan dive, the vertical farewell. They have no illusions, even if some try to use a jacket as a makeshift parachute. They take their chances. They escape. They are human because they decide to choose how they will die rather than allow themselves to be burned. One last manifestation of dignity: they will have chosen their end rather than waiting resignedly. Never has the expression "freefall" made more sense.

9:17

Bullshit, my dear Beigbeder. If somewhere between 37 and 50 people threw themselves from the top of the North Tower, it was simply because everything else was impossible, suffocation, pain, the instinct to survive, because jumping couldn't be worse than staying in this suffocating furnace. They jumped because it was not as hot outside as it was inside. Ask any firefighter, they'll tell you. Jumpers are people who have been pushed to the limits. They no longer have any sense of danger. Barely conscious, pumped up on adrenaline, they're so terrified, in such a state of shock that it's almost a state of ecstasy. You don't jump 1,300 feet because you're a free man. You jump because you're a hunted animal. You don't jump to preserve your humanity, you jump because the fire has reduced you to a brute beast. The void is not a rational choice. It's simply the only place that looks good from up there, somewhere you ache for, somewhere that doesn't slash your skin with white-hot claws, doesn't put out your eyes with searing-hot pokers. The void is a way out. The void is welcoming. The void stretches out its arms to you.

9:18

OK, CARTHEW, IF YOU'RE GOING TO BE LIKE THAT, I'LL GO TO NEW York. I realize the Tour Montparnasse isn't the third World Trade Center tower. In any case, my life's like a disaster movie right now: at 9:18 A.M. this morning, my lover left me. Flaubert said: "I travel to verify my dreams." I need to verify my nightmare. In a suicidal gesture, I decide to take the Concorde. I remember that the supersonic plane, created by de Gaulle in the sixties but inaugurated under Giscard d'Estaing in 1976, has an irritating tendency to crash into hotels in the suburbs of Paris. So I booked my seat because I like to live dangerously. I'm an adventurer, an extreme sports buff. Price of the ticket? €6,000 one-way—the price of a Chanel dress. Obviously time travel is cheap. Because the Concorde flying Paris–New York is the machine imagined by H. G. Wells: it takes off at 10 A.M. and lands at 8 A.M.: before Amélie dumps me, to be precise. Three hours from now I'll be in New York two hours ago.

The time travel begins as soon as you walk into the seventies lounge. I think I'm writing about September 11, but actually I'm writing about the seventies: the decade that spawned the WTC, the Tour Montparnasse, and the Concorde, which links them, of which three two no longer exist. Air hostesses in beige uniforms with botoxed lips, salon-tanned stewards, white armchairs, padded walls like a psychiatric hospital, businessmen glued to their cell phones, businesswomen unsheathing their Palm Pilots: everything looks dated, like in *2001: A Space Odyssey*. 2001 was two years ago: Kubrick's seventies dream didn't come true. People don't travel to the Moon to the music of Strauss waltzes; instead Boeings skyscrape to the music of muezzins.

Through the window at Orly Airport, I come face to face with the supersonic. Its beak is even more hooked than mine. Blue Concorde logos insist that it is a source of great national pride—an endangered species. The other day, a Concorde lost its rudder in midflight. I board the minuscule cabin: the VIPs bow their heads. Since the Gonesse crash, technical hitches have been plentiful: engine failures, cabin damage—the seventies are slowly giving up the ghost, and I might wind up stuck there, in the years of my forgotten childhood. Furthermore, the plane is almost empty. You really have to be a kamikaze like me to climb aboard this delta-winged bird. Given that my bravado is somewhat limited, I'm already on my fifth miniature of Absolut. I slump into seat 2D. It's raining and I look completely gonzo, dead drunk on a stationary Concorde.

Stewardess: Sir, may I suggest a glass of Krug to accompany your caviar . . . ?

Me: Nnyesss, that would be most agreeable.

I'm disappointed to die trapped in something that feels like a budget hotel in the middle of an industrial estate, but at least I'll have made the most of it to the bitter end. To top it off, it's Iranian osetra: Islamic caviar!

You have to be absolutely crazy to blow 6K just to cut three hours off your flying time. Were the guys who invented this thing completely out to lunch, or did they really think that saving that sliver of time was worth burning the extra tons of fuel? Who were these sixties engineers? The world they dreamed of seems so obsolete . . . so twentieth century. . . . A smooth, white, high-speed, plastic world in which triangular planes thumb their noses at time zones. . . . No one believes in it anymore. . . . My bald neighbor yawns, reading *L'Express*. . . . Everything was invented back then, in the last optimistic era . . . answering machines . . . jet lag . . . news magazines. . . . It used to be really cool to complain about jet lag; nowadays it's so tacky nobody mentions it. . . . I'm drunk as a skunk as the Concorde takes off with an ear-splitting racket accompanied by some suspicious shuddering. . . . If I were a girl, all I'd have to do is jam my pussy against the armrest to have multiple orgasms. . . . I'm flattened into my seat like a pancake. . . . The in-flight magazine boasts: "The rated thrust of each engine is 38,050 lbs. . . ." I'm wondering whether I'm about to upchuck my caviar. . . . "The thrust to weight ratio of the plane is 1.66 times greater than that of a Boeing 747." . . . Thrust sounds like a midwife screaming: "Push, push." Excuse me, stewardess, but I think I'm about to caviarize the pressurized cabin. "This considerable thrust is obtained using a standard jet engine combined with afterburner reheat system designed to heat the exhaust fumes, speeding up their exit. This has the effect of increasing thrust by 17 percent." . . . I threw up everything into my paper bag. . . . I feign nonchalance as we break the sound barrier over the barrier of the Atlantic . . . In front of me, a liquid crystal display tells me we are flying at Mach 2. . . . I must look pretty green round the gills when we pierce the stratosphere at 1350 mph. . . . I'm incapable of being the efficient, multitasking decision-maker dreamed of by the (probably mustached, given the time) inventors of the Concorde. Maybe it's the booze, but I find the fact that they were in such a hurry heartbreaking. . . . Since the Americans were frolicking on the Moon, they had to find something else to do. . . . The French are childish. . . . They were adults, high-minded scientists, aeronautics specialists; and yet they were kids, 'ickle babies playing with their 'ickle toys. Now, the only place their plane stills flies is in the pages of this book.

9:19

ON TOP OF A ROCKY PEAK OF ARTIFICIAL STONE, A PAIR OF LOVERS hold hands.

"I always hated Tuesday. It's still the beginning of the week, but it's even more depressing than Monday," says the blonde in Ralph Lauren.

"I can't fucking believe they can't get us out of here," says the guy in Kenneth Cole. "You haven't got a couple of Advil?"

"Sorry, I took the last two when I got that lungful of burning carpet," says the blonde in Ralph Lauren. "It ripped my throat out."

The ventilation ducts were spitting clouds into the meeting room. Smoke rose from the carpet in fine wisps at first, and then in thick columns along the walls like mist over swampland, or will-o'-the-wisp designed by an Italian interior decorator.

"When I think you'll never get to see my home cinema system . . . plasma screen the size of Lake Superior," says the guy in Kenneth Cole.

"Yeah. Too bad . . . But don't be so negative, the firefighters will get here, it's only a matter of time," says the blonde in Ralph Lauren.

"George Soros pray for us!" says the guy in Kenneth Cole.

"Ted Turner, come to our aid!" says the blonde in Ralph Lauren.

They start to giggle and their laughter becomes a coughing fit. Or maybe they were coughing from the start.

"What's the difference between Microsoft and *Jurassic Park*?" asks the guy in Kenneth Cole.

"Don't know, but I bet it's pretty feeble."

"One is an over-rated high tech theme park based on prehistoric information and populated mostly by dinosaurs, the other is a Steven Spielberg movie."

This time she really does laugh. The guy in Kenneth Cole gets a fit of the giggles. He can't stop, he's choking on his own joke, he's turning purple. The blonde explodes as well, they're gasping for breath at the guy's gag. It's nervous laughter. I suppose if you're going to choke to death, you might as well be laughing. But they pull themselves together. The blonde takes off her jacket. Her striped blouse is half open. A thin gold chain hangs between her breasts with a little heart on the end. Just outside the windows, America is ablaze.

"Did you phone your mom?" asks the guy in Kenneth Cole.

"No," says the blonde in Ralph Lauren, "better not, no point in worrying her for nothing. Either we get out of here and I call her, or we don't and I don't. I mean, what do you want me to say to her?"

"Bye mom, I love you. Tell the family I love them too," says the guy in Kenneth Cole.

"You dumb asshole," says the blonde in Ralph Lauren.

* * *

He wasn't a stupid asshole. He sat down on the table. He'd taken his jacket off too. He was having difficulty breathing. He loved this woman. He didn't want to lose her. He didn't want her to suffer. He thought about the times he met her at the office, all the cafés, all those spur-of-the-moment drinks, all those hotel rooms. He thought about her velvety skin with its scent of moisturizer. His heart was beating not only from fear; he was capable of emotion. He felt that it was all over, that it would never come back. He slowly realized their affair would end here, in this room with its off-white walls. She was a ravishing blonde; he could imagine her as a child, her pink cheeks, her hair blown back, a corn-fed blonde running through a meadow in a flower-print dress, a field of wheat or rye, holding a kite, that kind of shit.

9:20

HAVING PICKED A PLANE THAT CONSTANTLY CRASHES AND THE DESTINATION most vulnerable to terrorist attacks, under normal circumstances, I should have been done for then and there.

Regardless of speed, taking a plane to New York City will never feel the same again. Once upon a time: a sense of weightlessness, a childlike enthusiasm, a mixture of fascination and jealousy, feigned tiredness masking excited trepidation, naïve wonder, a sense of adventure and that good old cliché "the electric energy of the Big Apple" galvanized by the lyrics of "New York, New York" ("I'm gonna be a part of it"; "If I can make it there / I'll make it anywhere"). Nowadays: a sense of being in a B-movie, paranoia, saccharine pity, a nonchalant air masking your absurd terror, an obsessive interest of every passerby—especially anyone with a beard or a mustache—intense awareness of the most minute details, a foretaste of the end of the world, unwarranted smugness at emerging alive when the plane finally lands.

Before we land, the stewardesses handed out green slips. All aliens are required to fill out the U.S. Immigration and Naturalization Service questionnaire:

- Do you have a mental disorder? ❐ YES ❐ NO
- Are you carrying drugs and/or arms? ❐ YES ❐ NO
- Are you seeking entry to engage in criminal or immoral activities? ❐ YES ❐ NO
- Have you ever been or are you now involved in espionage or sabotage; or in terrorist activities; or genocide; or between 1933 and 1945 were you involved, in any way, in persecutions associated with Nazi Germany or its allies? ❐ JA ❐ NEIN
- Have you ever sought immunity from prosecution in exchange for testimony? ❐ YES ❐ NO

Lucky break: there's no question asking: "Are you intending to write a novel about September 11?"

My advice: always reply in the negative. Something tells me that a YES might invite administrative complications.

The U.S. Department of Justice might want to add some new questions:

- Are you a pedophile? ❐ YES ❐ NO
- Are you a member of the Bin Laden family? ❐ YES ❐ NO
- Do you regularly masturbate in front of photographs of dismembered corpses? ❐ YES ❐ NO

- Do you smoke cigarettes? ❒ YES ❒ NO
- (if you're a woman)—Are you intending to blow the President of the United States under his desk? ❒ YES ❒ NO

I suppose you think I'm spitting in the soup again? I suppose you think I should be grateful for my rich-kid lifestyle and shut up? Sorry, I'm investigating the obliteration of the seventies. The utopia of the seventies is one in which the majority of Earthlings refuse to live. Three hours from Paris to New York, that's the time it takes to go from Paris to Marseille by TGV. Concorde is an AGV getting us nowhere. It's just one folly among many and hardly seems the most dangerous. But the Avion à Grande Vitesse embodies an ideology best symbolized by the Concorde's nose-up as it lands, that graceful tilt as though looking down its nose at those not on board.

There is a communist utopia; that utopia died in 1989. There is a capitalist utopia; that utopia died in 2001.

During the flight, I constantly harassed the stewardess: "Are we there yet? Jeez, it's a really long flight. . . . Hey, aren't we running late? I've got the feeling we're running late. No, it's just, you know, I'm the only one here not traveling on expenses. . . ."

At John Fitzgerald Kennedy Airport, a fluorescent sign indicates GATES 9–11. They really should change it; it's in questionable taste. We arrived on time; that is to say, before we left. It was raining as we left; I arrive in a rain of tears. Everything is more beautiful in the rain, which washes away nothing, especially not our sins. 8:25 A.M.: Amélie hadn't left me yet. I'd pretended to be pressed for time to annoy the flight crew, but it wasn't true.

I was in no hurry for it to be 9:18 again.

9:21

I'M SICK OF MY THROAT FEELING SORE. IT STINKS IN HERE. MY EYES are burning and my feet are really hot. I try not to cry, but the tears leak out anyway. David says Dad's just recharging his batteries before doing something, he says the reason he hasn't done anything yet is because "it's not easy steering a Corvette one-handed along the edge of the Grand Canyon with your foot on the gas while looking behind you at an erupting volcano as Cameron Diaz arrives swinging from a helicopter wire and John Malkovitch screams into a megaphone 'cos there's only ten seconds left before the A-bomb on the seabed explodes creating a tidal wave that will submerge New York where his kids are being held hostage by the President's doppelgänger in a bunker guarded by bloodthirsty dinosaurs reared in a top-secret thermonuclear dump by secret government agents." In other words, Dave's convinced Dad's some guy called Ultra-Dude who's gonna get reactivated.

I'm just shit-scared, and I'd really like to get outta here. Dad says we gotta listen to Anthony, and Anthony says we hafta stay here and not panic and that the rescue guys will come get us.

What really scares me is that Dad's even more shit-scared than me. Fuck, it really freaks me out when I get a nosebleed, I've always gotta keep pressing on it, that's one hand, and Dad's holding the other one, and we're just, like, staring at this door, it's really creepy. Jeffrey's praying in Hebrew and Tony's praying in Arabic, I swear, it's pretty weird. But the craziest thing about it (apart from David thinking he's in some Marvel comic), is Dad's prayer.

"Oh Lord, I know I've kind of abandoned you lately, but there's the parable about the prodigal son, right? That's a really useful parable; if I understand it right, it means that even heathens and deserters will be welcomed with open arms if they come back to you, so, anyway, I'm feeling pretty prodigal this morning."

"See? Toldya he was gonna turn it super something," shouts David.

"Shut up, Jeez, Dad's trying to pray, it's holy."

All three of us hold hands and Dad keeps on praying.

"Lord, I'm weak and I've sinned and I ask forgiveness. Yes, I got divorced, it was my fault, my grievous fault. I left my family, my two sons who are here with me . . ."

"Stop, Dad, don't say that . . . Dad, stop, please . . ."

He's really freaking me out, oh shit, it's no use, I'm gonna cry. I try concentrating really hard on this blotch on the floor, but I just start sniveling. Fuck, this is hard. I just wanna be somewhere else. I want to be a fly flying around on the other side of this door. If someone told me that someday I'd be jealous of a fly . . . But no shit, it'd be really cool to be some random fly, you get to fly round and you don't get nosebleeds, a fly is free and it can fuck off and it doesn't think about stuff. I'd go BZZZ round the towers with my compound eyes and I'd look at all those assholes the other side of the windows, BZZZ and whaddya know, I flick my wings and I'm outta here without a second thought. That'd be dope.

"Oh God, I'm a selfish pig, but on my knees I beg you to forgive me . . ."

A deaf fly would be best.

9:22

In New York, I'm free, I can go wherever I want, pass myself off as whoever I want. I'm anyone: I'm everyman. I have no roots tying me down, no media mini-celebrity to fence me in. Fame, like relationships or old age, makes you predictable. Freedom is being single, young, and completely unknown. In my whole life I've never been as free as I am now: a solitary individual in a foreign city with money in my pocket. And what good is it? It's a hollow freedom. Since I can do anything, I do nothing. I get drunk in my hotel room, watch X-rated movies with the sound turned down because Mylène Farmer is asleep in the next room. I get depressed in designer bars. It's gotten to the point that when people ask how I am, I avert my eyes and change the subject, turning away so as not to cry. A simple "How are you?" is terrifying. "Everything OK?" sounds like a trick question.

The last time my fiancée left me, I didn't take her seriously because she's always leaving me. But this time is definitely the last, I can feel it. This time she won't come back and I'll have to learn to live without her when what I'd planned was the reverse: to die with her.

I hadn't loved her enough, now she didn't love me anymore. Women often take the initiative; I've no intention of suffering in silence:

"You were the greatest love of my life."

"I loathe past-tense declarations of love."

I've lived with women since I left my mother. Now, I'll have to get used to living on my own like my father. I wish my life was more complicated. Sadly, life is humiliating in its simplicity: we do everything we can to be rid of our parents; then we become them.

The stock market is plummeting. The Dow will soon be 7,000, 6,500, lower? Unemployment is rising. New York City is bankrupt (it has a 3.6-billion-dollar-deficit)—quick, start a war, get the economy moving. Every TV channel talks about bombing raids in Iraq. In return, every New Yorker waits for a nuclear terrorist attack. In the schools, children are given leaflets explaining how to seal doors with insulating tape in case of a chemical attack. Many families have equipped themselves with survival kits: flashlights and spare batteries, rope, water, iOSAT pills (medically developed to protect against radiation sickness). The yellow alert has been raised to an orange alert. And me, I'm wandering the streets of a threatened city looking for my navel.

Every decade brings with it a new illness. The eighties: AIDS. The nineties: schizophrenia. The 00s: paranoia. A single suicide bomber in the subway station at Times Square would be enough to trigger mass panic. But there have been no attacks in the United States since September 11. Americans should feel reassured by this. But no. Every day that goes by without a terrorist attack makes it more likely that there will be one. Alfred Hitchcock said it again and again: terror is mathematical. This morning, the Americans arrested Khalid Shaikh Mohammed, one of the brains behind Al Qaeda. They should feel reassured by this. But, no: the government braces itself for reprisals.

It's insane how much at home I feel in the most threatened city on earth. Terrorism is a permanent sword of Damocles, punch holes in buildings. I'm in my element here. In any case, without you, nowhere is bearable. When you are dragging your own Judgment Day around, you might as well be somewhere apocalyptic.

What did I come here to find? Me.

Will I find myself?

9:23

Terrorism does not destroy symbols, it hacks people of flesh and blood to pieces. All these commingled tears. Jeffrey's, Jerry's, mine. David, thankfully, lives in his own imaginary world. He has good reason to shrink from hostile reality. Lourdes brings bottles of Evian she's found who knows where. God bless her. We fall on them. With all the smoke we've inhaled, the fumes and the fuel, we're close to asphyxia, but we're extremely dehydrated too. It's at this point that Anthony has an asthma attack. Poor guy rolls around on the floor and we don't know what to do to help. I feel distraught. Lourdes pours mineral water into his mouth but he coughs it right back up. Jeffrey gestures to me and we carry Anthony downstairs to the restrooms on the floor below. I take his legs and Jeff holds him by the armpits (one of his arms has been severely burned). Again I entrust Jerry and David to Lourdes. Anthony struggles to inhale, to exhale. I'm shaking like a fucking idiot; Jeffrey is calmer, more collected. He puts Anthony's head under the faucet. Anthony vomits something black. I take some paper towels from the machine to wipe his face. When I turn back, Jeffrey's holding Anthony's head against his chest. Anthony isn't moving.

"Is he . . . dead?"

"Fuck, I don't know, I'm not a doctor. He's not breathing, I think maybe he just passed out."

He shakes Anthony, slaps him. He doesn't like the idea of giving mouth-to-mouth (because of the vomit): so I'm the one who takes charge. It's useless. Silence. I tell Jeffrey we have to leave him here, that he might come round, that I've got to get back to my kids. He shakes his head.

"You don't get it—this guy was our only hope of getting out of here. It's over. We've let him die, and pretty soon we'll be joining him."

I opened the restroom door. I think: wow, the three-ply toilet paper matches the pink marble. I have time to notice even this. My brain keeps hoarding insignificant details when I've got better fucking things to do.

"I've gotta go."

I never saw Jeffrey again. My last image I have of him, he's sitting on the gray tiles smoothing Anthony's hair. The pink door closes. I rush back to the kids. I jostle people who, like me, are wandering aimlessly trying to find shelter, an exit, a smoke-free lounge, a way out of the labyrinth. But there's no "no smoking area" in Tower One this morning. This isn't L.A.

I'd like to have done that: made jokes, said "Fuck it" and just given up, but I couldn't. I didn't have the right. I was convinced that I had to save my kids; though in fact they were the ones who saved me, since they stopped me from giving up. The soles of my shoes were sticking to the floor like they had chewing gum on them: I think they were starting to melt.

9:24

To me, New York was the wOOOO-wOOOO of sirens contrasting with the French NEE-naw. That dazzling extra light that makes them seem serious, that scares you shitless. New York: a city where they speak 80 languages. The victims of the attack were of 62 different nationalities.

First thing I do when I arrive: tell the taxi driver to take me to Ground Zero.

"You mean the World Trade Center site?"

New Yorkers don't like to say "Ground Zero." The driver heads down to the end of the city and drops me in front of a fence. At 9:24, New York is a wire fence hung with photos of the missing, candles, wilting bouquets. A black plaque enumerates the names of the "heroes" (the victims). The more exact term would be: the martyrs. In fact, a cross has been planted at the memorial, even though not all the dead were Christians. . . . Flowers strew the snow-covered ground. It's very cold: fifteen degrees below zero Celsius. "Less than Zero": I think briefly of Bret Easton Ellis. Less than Ground Zero. I go into One World Financial Center, the only building in the neighborhood still standing. No search, no security checks, I could be caked with dynamite. In the Winter Garden, under a glass dome inspired by the Crystal Palace in London, I walk toward the picture window that looks directly onto the gaping hole. Ground Zero: a crater filled with bulldozers. Thousands of workers have already begun rebuilding. On the ground floor, the various architectural submissions are displayed. Daniel Libeskind's proposal won the competition: the tallest tower in the world, four crystals forming a U surrounding a bathtub, like a smashed piece of quartz. No one would want to blow it up: it's already in pieces. Pity: I really liked the World Cultural Center project submitted by THINK Design. The other side of the World Financial Center overlooks the sea, the wind, the spray, and a branch of Starbucks.

I note the presence of a number of garbage cans. French police clearly haven't informed local authorities about the modus operandi of Islamic terrorists in Paris: nail bombs in garbage cans, that kind of thing . . . For some time now in France we've learned to live with fear in our bellies. Over here, there are cops with shades and walkie-talkies everywhere, but they still have too much faith in mankind. A hundred feet from Ground Zero, the Pussycat Lounge (96 Greenwich Street) and its naked creatures attest to the fact that life goes on. One vodka and tonic later, I walk past the Federal Reserve, where 22,285,376 pounds of gold are stored eighty feet below ground. Then I wander into St. Paul's church, which is miraculously unscathed: it dates from 1762. An exhibition pays tribute to the rescue services: photos of the missing, objects found in the rubble are lined up in glass cases, tubes of toothpaste, diapers, bandages, candy, a crucifix, sheets of paper and hundreds, thousands, of children's drawings. I bring my hand to my mouth. I no longer feel sorry for myself. Here in the midst of this terribly saccharine suffering stood a cynic in tears.

Later still, a little farther uptown, at the Carousel Café, another strip joint, a dancer wearing a thong tells me that in the weeks following the eleventh the Salvation Army came twice a day to get ice so they could serve cold drinks to the families of the victims at the Armory, and to rescuers working in the oppressive heat of the smoldering site.

"When the club opened again a week after the attack, the girls couldn't believe it: it was full of blue-collar workers dead on their feet who snapped up the free drinks, and us, too! They wanted to talk. There were ambulances and fire trucks screaming all the time outside the door. Everything was burning. These guys needed something to take their minds off things. I remember when I'd bend down to pick up my clothes, they were caked in white dust."

9:25

RESTAURANTS COOK UP ALL KINDS OF STUFF, JUST USUALLY NOT THE customers. Up here, we're the barbecue. Dad came back with a face six feet long. Lourdes looked at him inquisitively and he shook his head.

"Anthony stayed downstairs with Jeffrey," he said, hoping David and me wouldn't understand. I don't know about Dave, but I know exactly what the score is. We're trapped in this tower with no way of going up or down. And this hellacious heat. I'm so totally boiling I can't think about anything else. I figure I'm too young to die. I want to study astronomy and investigate the stars with my telescope and be an astronaut with NASA so I can float up there above the blue planet. It's cooler in space.

I really need to take a piss so I let go Dad's hand—he's trying to explain to Dave that he's not Batman.

"But if you were Batman you'd still say you weren't Batman," David says.

"Where you going?" Dad asks me.

"I hafta go pee," I answer.

"Wait . . . don't . . ."

Too late, I run down the smoky corridor and bang! I come across Anthony lying on the floor and Jeffrey standing looking at himself in the mirror.

"Is he dead or what?"

"No, he's asleep."

"What the hell are you doing?"

"Thinking."

"OK, well while you're thinking I have to go pee."

But I couldn't pee. I tried and tried but it wouldn't come. Happens to me sometimes, I can't pee when there's people around. Jeez, I look like a complete schmuck.

"C'mon, you gonna piss or what?" said Jeffrey.

"I can't. I'm stuck."

"Yeah, well I'm stuck too, we're all stuck."

I zip up my fly. I did my best to put up a good show but Jeffrey could tell I'd been crying. We just stood there staring at each other. Jeffrey kept on starting sentences I couldn't make out: "There's too much . . . I didn't . . . I was the one who brought them all . . . What are we gonna . . . I can't . . ." I could tell he needed to talk but he couldn't do it. That's when I pissed my pants.

When I left the john, Dad was there, and he had David in his arms, and I was mega glad he was there. He carried us back to the emergency exit. I told him Anthony was resting and Jeffrey had gone down.

"What d'you mean 'gone down'?"

"He said he was gonna do some stuff for the guys from his work, then he left. He was really weird. He was talking about going through the windows to get down. You think that's possible?"

Dad looked nervous. He could tell I'd peed my pants but he didn't say anything. Lucky for me 'cos otherwise David would have ragged me, like, forever. Soon as I got a nosebleed, he'd be right in there.

"Kids, I don't think we're gonna see Jeffrey again."

9:26

I ORDER A WHITE WINE AT PASTIS, THE HIP RESTAURANT RUN BY Keith McNally, who already owns another French restaurant, Balthazar. I like the decor, it's perfect—a French brasserie re-created right in the middle of Soho. I told the woman I love that I had to go to New York alone; that's what gave her the idea of dumping me for good. People think my life is funny, but it's not. I can't stick at anything. I got married, I got divorced. I had a kid, but I don't parent. I'm in love, I run away to New York. I'm handicapped, and I'm not the only one. I live in a no-man's-land: neither an INTERNATIONAL PLAYBOY nor MARRIED AND PROUD OF IT. I'm indecisive and no one feels sorry for me. I'm fucked up and I've no right to complain. I have a crippled heart: like the song by Enrico Macias, *"Le Mendiant de l'Amour."* Still, it's amazing how many thirtysomethings I know are in the same boat. Emotional cripples. Grown, vaccinated men behaving like kids. Underneath the dashing exterior is an emotional cripple. With no memories, no plans. They want to be like their fathers, and at the same time they're determined not to end up like their fathers, no matter what. Their father abandoned them and they never found him. It's not a criticism: I blame society. The sons of 1968 are men with no role models. Men with no instruction manual. Men with no solidity. Defective men. When they're in a relationship, they're smothered; when they're single, they're miserable. Even their psychoanalyst is lost; he doesn't know what else to tell them. There's no example for them to follow. There's no solution to the tragedy of my generation. I'm someone who only enjoys beginnings, and I've forgotten my childhood. I'm someone who only enjoys beginnings, and I don't look after my child. For thousands of years we did things differently. Mom and Dad and their kids lived in the same house. Barely forty years ago, we decided to do away with the father, and we want things to carry on as before? I'm the product of that disappearing father. I am collateral damage.

One morning, at 9:26 A.M., I realized that I was incapable of loving anyone except myself. The day was my mirror. In the morning, I thought about what I was going to say on TV. In the afternoon, in front of the cameras, I said what I had to say. In the evening I watched myself on TV saying it. Sometimes I'd see myself four times, because it would be repeated three times. The night before, I watched the rough edit of a different program for seven hours on the trot. I spent all my time admiring my own face on a color screen, but even that wasn't enough. I called my friends before the show to remind them when it started; I called them afterward to make sure they'd watched it. I organized drinks parties where I left the TV on so that we could—as I said with feigned irony—"watch me in concert."

* * *

I blame the consumer society for making me what I am: insatiable. I blame my parents for making me what I am: vague.

I blame other people to avoid blaming myself.

No memories of my childhood. Fragments, an image or two. I'm jealous of people who can recount every detail of their life as a baby. I remember nothing, a few flashes, which I copy down here in no particular order, nothing more. I believe that I didn't begin to exist until 1990, when I published my first book: a memoir, coincidentally. Writing restored my memory to me.

For example, there's Verbier, my father's chalet, in 1980. It was a man's house. I like our vacations together, just guys skiing. Every night we pig out on fondue, and there are no chicks around to complain about our diet. I light the fire in the hearth, Charles skis until it's dark, Dad reads the American papers. And every morning he wakes us, my brother and me, by tickling our feet, which stick out from under the Ikea duvet, trying to make up for the fact for our first fifteen years of our lives he wasn't there to do it.

And another one: when I was ten I started keeping a travel diary on a beach in Bali (Indonesia) between water fights with my big brother while Dad hit on sun-drenched girls at the hotel bar. I didn't know that I would never stop putting my life down on paper. That little green notebook: a gear still grinding inside me.

I decided to research myself. Rather than wait for Proustian flashes of "involuntary memory," I become a reporter, I retrace my steps.

* * *

I have no memory of Neuilly-sur-Seine. Nonetheless, I was born there. In a small white private hospital. I'm from the well-heeled suburbs. That's probably where I get my expensive tastes. I like cleanliness, neat gardens, soundless cars, nursery schools where they shoot the first hostages straight away. German governesses, whom we refer to, however, as "nurses." I see childhood as something pristine, sleek, and, for the most part, boring as hell.

I was born with silver spoon up my ass. I'd love to tell you about the anguished childhood of an accursed artist. I envy Dave Pelzer: my life wasn't tragic. It's tragic how little tragedy there was.

I wasn't a wanted child. Born seventeen months after my brother I'm one of those cases—common at the time—of an unplanned second pregnancy. The boy who arrives too early. It's hardly a news story: the pill wasn't legal in 1965, most children arrived unplanned. But two children make a lot more racket than one. I have to admit that in my father's shoes, I'd have done exactly what he did: get the fuck out and fast! In fact, thirty-three years later, that's precisely what I did.

I wasn't on the agenda. That's how it goes; no big deal, human beings coped with such things for thousands of years. Anyway, when I finally did show up, I was lucky: I was pampered, mollycoddled, spoiled rotten; it would be churlish to bitch. It's either too much love or not enough. I not going to go and do a Romain Gary and complain about how my mother loved me too much! It's very important to be traumatized by one's parents. We need it. We are all traumatized children who traumatize their own. I'd rather be traumatized by my parents than by someone I didn't know.

Anyway, there I was just the same, squatting my own life. I'd invited myself to this planet. Someone had to set another place at the table for me; sorry, there'll be less dessert for everyone. For a long time I've had the feeling that I am a burden to others. Hence my taste for parasitism: my life is a party where I showed up without an invite.

I discovered that television was a way to make myself desired. I wanted crowds on their knees begging me to exist. I wanted hordes of fans pleading with me to show up. I wanted to be chosen, celebrated, a celebrity. It's ridiculous, isn't it, the little twists of fate that make us work flat out instead of being normal?

9:27

The great thing about Candace was her "hasbian" side: an ex-lesbian knows her body better and knows exactly how to touch it to make herself come. Women who haven't slept with other women are not nearly as good in bed, same as men who aren't bi. What am I doing thinking about sex instead of how to save our asses? Because it is a way of saving our asses. As long as I am a sex maniac, I am. When I stop thinking about sex, I will cease to be. Jerry looks at me the way he looks at life in general: with a benevolence that is, however, belied by the facts. Is that what love is? Kindness that is completely unjustified?

"What are we gonna do, Dad?"

"I don't know. Wait here, there's no point going back down."

"Any minutes now," says Lourdes, "they're gonna land rescue teams on the roof. They'll break this door down and we'll be the first ones out of here."

"Really? Maybe there's too much smoke for them to land."

"They don't need to land no helicopters, just drop a couple of cops and firefighters and their gear onto the roof at the end of a rope. Chrissakes, they're trained for this kinda situation . . ."

Lourdes has found hope again, that's the most important thing. At least one of us has to muster some self-assurance at all times in this cramped, claustrophobic hole. Hope is like a witness, like a tank of oxygen which we pass around among ourselves.

"Are they gonna jump down onto the roof in, like, those black suits and masks and stuff?" Jerry asks.

"Well, duh!" says David. "They're not gonna come dressed as Mickey and Donald and Goofy."

"A good team with a blowtorch, they'd have this door open in less than three minutes, even with the lock broken."

"Maybe they'll be able to hack into the security system and unlock it, like Tom Cruise in *Mission: Impossible*."

"Wow, yeah, like suspended on cables upside down. Too cool!"

We need something to believe in. Lourdes and Jerry start praying, droning "God save us, please save us," hands joined, looking up at the filthy ceiling of our prison. For now, at least, we're still alive.

9:28

DISASTERS ARE BENEFICIAL: THEY MAKE PEOPLE WANT TO LIVE. NEW York in the 00s is like Paris in the twenties after the slaughter of World War I. The Roaring Twenties was a riot of champagne, and Americans came to Paris to live it up. Since September 11, the wild times are in New York and the French come here to be insulted. In fact I put on a Spanish accent so people will leave me alone:

"Olé! Está magnífico! Muy muy caliente! Sí sí sí, señorita."

Dazed New Yorkers mistake me for an ally. The Big Apple is the forbidden fruit into which every Eve sinks her perfect white teeth. The planes have created a huge brothel. Am I being over-optimistic? The city is still in mourning; maybe that's why everyone is wearing black. Only a handful of resistance fighters drown their sorrows in parties and live as if nothing had changed. But everything's changed, as I'll soon realize. It's just that I only hang out with ornery people.

For example, by 9:28 P.M., on the Lower East Side at Idlewild, boys and girls are dancing topless. The girls have flowers painted on their breasts. This is something they call "swinging lite": there's a lot of caressing, kissing, fondling, but no penetration. There are lots of such parties, Cake being the most famous.

"It's not an orgy!" says the mistress of the house. "Just an erotic soirée."

Often, a couple will leave with someone of random gender, and you can't get them on the phone for two days . . . but there are also lots of guys who just get off on watching their girlfriend French-kissing another girl, and nothing more. Cover charge: $50 for a couple, $15 for a woman on her own. Careful: the parties tend to finish early so everyone can head off somewhere else to fuck. The aim of these new parties is to move beyond fidelity, to think outside the couple, to invent different ways of loving without sacrificing desire.

New York is the only place in the world where you can still find that rarest of creatures: girls wearing sandals in winter drinking pink cocktails from triangular glasses and swaying to Craig David. Recipe for a Cosmopolitan: Absolut Citron, Cointreau, cranberry juice, and lime served in a martini glass. This treacherous tipple reminds me of the Tonios of my youth in Irùn (gin, vodka, grenadine, orange juice): ghastly memories of my first drunken outings with some sugary mixture in my veins. I have a drink or five. Bin Laden wishes these girls harm. I wish them well, with their nipples hard in their tight crop-tops. And it's at this point that I have an epiphany. Today's INTERNATIONAL PLAYBOY is a woman. It's Bridget Jones or Carrie Bradshaw (the heroine of *Sex and the City*). These are the people the fanatical Muslims are scared of, and I can understand why. They scare me shitless too, with their heavy artillery: mascara, lip gloss, oriental perfumes, silk lingerie. They've declared war on me. They terrify me because something tells me that I'll never be able to seduce them all. There's always another one on the horizon, heels higher than the last. It's an impossible task. If they crashed a charter plane onto the city every day, they still wouldn't succeed in eradicating the bevy of dangerous beauties; the sexual imperialism of these sumptuous sluts in their I ESCAPED THE BETTY FORD CLINIC T-shirts; the supremacy of their devastating necklines and their eyelashes, which flutter as they contemptuously write you off: "You're not on my to-do list. Stop hitting on me, man. I do the hunting tonight. Scram! Beat it!"

"Coffee and a taxi please." (I suppose you think your tits and your legs do something for me. Apart from giving me a boner, zilch. So shut the fuck up, you and your sandals. Not even close.)

Does pleasure replace fear? Fanatics are hitting the fan. Their terrorization has produced precisely the reverse of what they had hoped. Hedonism is at its peak. Babylon lives again! Women aren't veiling their faces; on the contrary, they're stripping in restaurants, play blind man's buff, making out with co-workers and kissing strange boys at "speed-dating" evenings. A new Jazz Age gets under way in an excess of debauchery while we bomb foreign countries. People teasingly make out, and terrorism falls to pieces. Terrorism terrorizes no one: it shores up freedom. Sex dances with death. There are no winners, only losers like me. As I walk into a transsexual Chinese cabaret (Lucky Cheng's), they burst into a song to the tune of "Happy Birthday to You": "Happy Blow-job to you! Happy Blow-job to you!"

Polygamous, dope-smoking beardy-weirdos want to give us lessons in morality? OK, guys, you win, we'll all live like you: we'll all be polygamous and smoke dope. There's time enough later to be disillusioned. We laugh ourselves silly one minute, next minute we're miserable. That's how we live.

9:29

For three-quarters of an hour now there's been a plane under our feet, when suddenly Jerry says he'd like to be a fly.

"Doofus!" says David. "Ever see a fly against a window? They fly around like crazy and never find the way out."

"He's right, Jerry. You don't need to become a fly, you're already a fly and so am I, and Dave here is a mosquito. C'mon, let's go buzz buzz against the windows."

And I start buzzing like a wasp running around in all directions. Lourdes looks worried. Jerry looks flabbergasted. Finally, I'm rewarded: David laughs and starts twisting his napkin into little feelers on his head. Lourdes claps as Jerry joins us and we all buzz around bouncing off the walls. Anthony picked a good spot. This room is relatively sheltered from the rest of the tower as long as we keep the doors sealed. Lourdes presses her ear against the door to the roof. She tells us to shut up on a regular basis, so that she can listen for helicopters dropping firefighters on the roof. But all we hear is the screeching of the girders as they buckle, the screams of the burning, and the dull, oppressive rumble of the fire. David the mosquito starts the buzzing again, stinging his brother with his finger, and off we go again.

Another minute killed.

9:30

THE AMERICAN "GRAND TOUR" HAS BEEN A GREAT FRENCH TRAdition since Chateaubriand and his nephew (by marriage) de Tocqueville. We enjoy contemplating the vastness of America with sardonic fascination. In the nineteenth century it was romanticism and squaws. In the twentieth century, the birth of global capitalism and the consumer society (the New York of Paul Morand and Louis-Ferdinand Céline). In the twenty-first, it's clear that the system no longer runs smoothly, that if we want to understand our own annihilation, we have to walk back up Broadway in the rain. Overstressed executives sit slumped on wooden frames on the sidewalk in the shelter of cinema posters, having their shoulders massaged. The sex shops have been replaced with Disney stores. The LED Coca-Cola billboards are on the blink: the bloodred logo flashes nervously like a broken strobe. What is this sodden crowd searching for? Money is no longer their God. Céline walked this same boulevard in 1925; he evokes it in 1932 in *Journey to the End of the Night*: "It's a district filled with gold, a miracle, and through the doors you can actually hear the miracle, the sound of dollars being crumpled, for the Dollar is always too light, a genuine Holy Ghost, more precious than blood." It's not the same anymore; we no longer worship hard cash, people are sick and tired of it but they don't know any other way of living, so they get a neck rub, stretch out on couches, cheat on their wives with their mistresses and on their mistresses with guys; they search for love, buy vitamin tablets, step on the gas, honk their horns—yeah, that's the universal sign of despair—they honk their horns so people will know they exist.

The history between France and America is long dormant. Perhaps it's time to wake it up. France can still help; my country could be useful for something for once. France is not America's mother—that's England—but it could claim to be America's godmother. You know, the crusty old aunt with the facial hair problem you only see on big family occasions—her breath stinks, you're a bit ashamed of her, more often than not you forget she exists—but who reminds you of her existence from time to time by giving you a beautiful gift.

Walking down Madison Avenue, I meet a girl with a black cross outlined on her forehead. Then another. Then two bankers bearing the same cross on their foreheads. I begin to think I'm seeing things, but I didn't have anything to drink at lunch. There are dozens of them now, tall and short, VPs and PAs, all walking around with a cross tattooed on their foreheads in soot. I'm convinced there's some madman a couple of blocks away distracting their attention and smearing black paint on their foreheads when they're not looking. The sidewalk is packed with people with crosses on their faces. I swim against the tide of urban crossbreeds and finally I realize: they're coming from Saint Patrick's Cathedral. Today is Ash Wednesday. There's a line several blocks long hanging around waiting to have holy ashes applied to their foreheads. It gives you an idea of the atmosphere in the capital of the world. Workers from every walk of life are willing to give up their lunch hour so that a priest can draw a cross on their foreheads in dust. I've never seen the like of it in France.

Something else is new: New Yorkers have become unbelievably considerate, helpful, thoughtful, polite. I remember the fanatical individualism of the eighties, when you'd see a New Yorker stepping over the corpse of a homeless person on the sidewalk without breaking stride. There's nothing like that now. Firstly, because Giuliani's relocated all the homeless (or they're dead); but something else has happened: apocalyptic politeness. The end of the world makes people kind. I saw someone help a blind man across the road in the snow, a woman pick up a man's umbrella, two people hail the same taxi and each suggest the other take this one. It's like a Frank Capra movie! Ten, twenty times a day I've spotted this strange hybrid, this mutant creature, this incredible thing: a philanthropic New Yorker.

September 11 has had two diametrically opposed consequences: kindness at home, cruelty abroad.

9:31

My name's David Yorston and my Dad's about to mutate. He keeps saying he's not a superhero, but the transformation is imminent. Two minutes ago, he was imitating a fly: the signs are unmistakable.

"David, I'm not Superman! I wish I was! You think I'm proud of just being me?"

A typical denial. Mortals with superhuman powers always pretend to be puny humans so they can preserve their freedom of movement and autonomy of action. There's a really strong smell of chocolate. Yummy.

"It's the candy machine on 108," says Lourdes, "starting to cook."

OK, now it's starting to stink. Dad's walking round in circles like a mutant in a cage. That's when he spots the camera: a little gray box dangling from the ceiling. He rushes at it waving his arms.

"Hey! Yoo-hoo! We're up here!"

He holds Jerry up to the camera, then lifts me up too. He's squeezing me so hard he's bruising my arms. It's probably his superpowers getting activated.

"They can see us! Hello! Come and get us!"

He jumps up and turns the camera toward the door and points at it.

"Look at the door! OPEN THE DOOR!"

Dad's doing the pogo, he looks like the Chili Peppers all rolled into one.

But little cameras like that don't have microphones, so there's no point screaming your head off.

Several hundred feet below, in the deserted Command Center, on one of the hundreds of black and white monitors on the video wall, a forty-year-old man appears, waving, flanked by his two children and a mute woman with coffee-colored skin who sits with her back to the wall. The other security monitors show deserted offices with broken windows, blocked elevators piled with blackened corpses, smoke-filled corridors, lobbies flooded by sprinklers, stairwells filled with hundreds of people walking down single file, passing hundreds of breathless firefighters walking up. On the console in front of empty chairs, thousands of red lights blink. Sirens howl uselessly. If God exists, I wonder what the fuck he was doing that day.

9:32

I APPROACHED EVERYONE I MET AND ASKED THEM THE SAME question:

"Have you been to Windows on the World?"

And everyone looked at me, suspicious, disconcerted.

"Why bring up that tragedy again?"

Coming from a Frenchman, the question seemed obscene, voyeuristic. I was trying to resurrect a phantom restaurant. The Ghost Diner. So I went back to my Spanish accent.

"Pero que está muy intéresante and I lova youra countrya. Penélope Cruz, she's hot, no? Olé olé!"

Several New Yorkers assure me that they no longer enjoy blue skies over the city. Good weather is no longer synonymous with peace here. With a nod to Hunter S. Thompson, I could have called this book *Fear and Loathing in New York.* The Department of Homeland Security advises the public to buy plastic sheeting and rolls of insulating tape to block air vents in case of attacks with chemical or biological weapons.

Today, I continue my visit, walking along the Hudson as far as the huge aircraft carrier docked at Pier 86: the *Intrepid*. On November 25, 1944, it was attacked by two Japanese kamikaze fighters. Now it has been transformed into the *Intrepid* Sea-Air-Space Museum. In fact, what we're dealing with is the center of military-patriotic propaganda. On the entrance, I read the motto of the U.S. Air Force: AIM HIGH. Films to the glory of the U.S. Army are projected in front of a sparse audience: kids sucking Popsicles and a few skeptical Japanese. The reason I've come: a piece of the fuselage of American Airlines Flight 11 is displayed in a glass case in the belly of the aircraft carrier. I approach the relic shyly. The display is very solemn. In a Plexiglas cube, a number of ruined objects have been carefully placed on a layer of gray powder collected at Ground Zero: a crushed laptop, sheets of photocopied paper stained with dried blood. And in the center of the case, a scorched steel plate measuring about three feet square: I stand before what remains of the Boeing that crashed below Windows on the World. It's a scratched, blackened, twisted piece of metal. At the center, you can make out an oval-shaped hole in the melted aluminum: the window. The visitors gather in front of this window onto ashes. Window on the dust. I lean over, a few bare inches from Flight 11, if the glass were not there, I could touch the first plane of September 11.

I have never been closer to carnage.

9:33

HOW JESUS DIDN'T SAVE ME

THE MEMORY OF MOM'S APPLE PIE, THE SMELL CREEPING UP THE stairs to wake me, still lying in bed. Under a sky orange as a chimney we drive along in our car, a small metal box under the stars. We used to take long trips across Texas, the largest state in the Union, Dad at the wheel, Mom sleeping, and us in the back snoring, except me. I was just pretending. I was listening to those bulky eight-track cartridges—remember them?—like cassettes big as paperbacks. You could skip from one song to another. Dad was listening to "Drive My Car" from the Beatles' *Rubber Soul,* and in my head I was humming "bee-beep, bee-beep, yeah!" Or maybe it was the Doors, *L.A. Woman*, that begins with the incredible blues song "The Changeling." Eyes closed, I moved my head to the rhythm, scared that Dad would fall asleep at the wheel which is why in my head I was shouting, "Wake up, Dad!"

"Dad, wake up! Wake up, Dad!"

I recognize my son's voice.

"Huh? Was I asleep long?"

Lourdes explains that I fainted, passed out for a minute. The kids are drowsy, flushed like me. The toxic fumes must be getting to us without our realizing. I'd like to go back to sleep, back to the dream of my childhood, my family. I'm beginning to love my family the way you love an inflatable dinghy in a storm. Lourdes starts talking; it's her turn. She never managed to have children, she says, that's why she wants to help with Jerry and David. She says they don't need her down in the restaurant. She says we have to stay calm, that we'll get through this, that we just have to wait, and I get the feeling that she's absolutely convinced of it. She manages to get a signal on her cell phone and phones her brother, who's sick with worry. She tells him what I told Mary: tell the rescue services that we're on the roof, that we're fine but the smoke is getting worse, we don't really know where to go . . . she doesn't reassure him.

The woman is a saint. Every day, we rub shoulders with saints without realizing. She goes through her pockets and takes out a pack of chewing gum which she passes round in silence. We put them in our mouth as though they were communion hosts. Then the boys start playing with her again.

I deliberately chose to desert my own flesh and blood. These two brats were holding me back. I can't help thinking any man who stays with a woman for more than three years is a coward and a liar. I wanted to say "Fuck you" to middle-class ideas of the perfect family: that a man shouldn't leave the mother of his children even if he's in love with another woman, that if he does, he's a bastard, an asshole with no sense of responsibility. A "sense of responsibility" clearly meaning cheating on your wife without her finding out. I didn't agree. Real responsibility is telling your children the truth, not some phony, hypocritical bullshit. These days, so-called laid-back, liberal society imposes a cardboard cutout of love as a model of stability. The sixties were a "magical detour." What I wanted to tell my sons was that you should never stay with someone you don't love; that you should be faithful to love and love alone; that you should tell society to piss off as often as possible. I wanted to tell them that a father's love for his children is indestructible and has nothing to do with whether their Dad loves their Mom. I wanted to tell them what my father never told me, because his father never told him: I love you. I love you but I'm free. I love you, but Christianity can go fuck itself. You are the only people I will love for more than three years.

Now, here I was all choked up like some schmuck, marveling at them, wrapping myself up in the most reactionary archetype in the world, sitting on a furnace, all warm and snug, and soon we were going to die together, and I realized I'd been wrong about everything.

9:34

At 9:34 a.m. in the offices of Cantor Fitzgerald the employees scuttled under their steel desks, each to their own little corner, to burn to a cinder. We don't know whether the fifty people in the conference room prayed, but they used the word "God" a lot on the cell phones. On the 92nd floor at Carr Futures, they were up to their knees in water. Two dozen brokers were asphyxiated in a meeting room, piled up near the door like a gas chamber. On the 95th floor, the left wing of the plane had ripped out the ceiling, the walls, the windows, the information desk, even the marble in the reception area. It was pitch dark, blood flowed, there was a smell of singed hair; it was the silence of lifeless bodies. In the South Tower, at Keefe, Bruyette & Woods, the investment banking division took the stairs and survived; not the traders. They didn't want to miss the opening bell.

It's snowing over the city. On the sidewalks, a layer of white powder falls from the heavens as it did on the eleventh—though natural this time—and settles on the asphalt. From the observation deck of the Empire State Building, the city looks as though it's covered with a white sheet, like sofas in a sleeping country house. But here, there are police sirens and the murmur, the pulse of urban life. Few tourists have come here this morning; the icy wind whips the snowflakes, stinging the eyes. A loudspeaker broadcasts an Ella Fitzgerald song: "In my solituuuude, you hauuuunt me." The view is obscured, but if I try hard I can make out the rocks and the water, even the waves on the East River, circular ripples on the expanse of black. Above my head, the needle on the Empire State Building—intended as a place where airships could moor—looks like the mast on top of the Eiffel Tower, which Americans had wanted to outdo since 1899; which they finally succeeded in outdoing in 1931. I walk around the terrace: behind the curtain of snow, I can see chimneys smoking, as if New York were a rumbling forge, a factory with ten million workers. Over the mantle of white, several strata of gray are overlaid, like confectioner's sugar, then a sudden flash of orange—canvas sheeting around a building site; or gold—the dome of a building; or silver—the Chrysler Building in the distance, pearlescent in the cotton clouds. A pair of lovers asks me to take their photo. I despise them. Their lightheartedness hits me as hard as the cold air. I feel like grabbing the girl by her fur collar and screaming:

"Enjoy it while it lasts. One day he'll go to a brothel with his buddies and you'll cheat on him in a hotel room with someone from the office. You'll wind up leaving him, and who'll hold onto the photo I'm taking? Nobody. It's a waste of film; it'll end up in a shoebox at the back of a wardrobe."

In the world bitterness championships, I'm aiming to make the finals. But I don't say anything, of course, and I immortalize them, a kiss in the ice. Turning toward the south, I verify that the two towers are missing. The Empire State Building should be happy: it is once again the pinnacle of the city. For thirty years, two buildings attempted to contest its supremacy, but that's all over now: the seventies are dead. The Empire State, at 1,250 feet, is kingpin again. At every moment, the shifting light transforms the landscape. To the north, the Pan Am Building has changed its name: MetLife, I write your name. Similarly, the RCA Building is now the GE Building. The three things that change a skyline are: clouds, terrorist attacks, and branding.

9:35

THE BATTLE FOR THE AIR: STRUGGLING TO GET EVEN YOUR TORSO out the window, to escape the furnace—the lungs are insistent. Down in Windows on the World, Jeffrey helps his co-workers from the Risk Water Group to find pockets of air. Standing on the bar. In the kitchens, the freezer. Through the windows on the north face. The fire rages. A number of other executives have managed to get through to the Fire Department, who give them the same instructions: "Don't move, we're on our way." As if we *could* move. Jeffrey is looking for water, but nothing comes out of the faucets anymore, so he tips water out of a vase hanging from the ceiling to moisten his group's napkins. He tears down the red drapes to stanch, or at least to filter, the smoke. He waves tablecloths out the window where huddles of people are screaming for help. Jeffrey isn't scared anymore. He's become a hero. He upends tables over puddles of water so his friends can cross the corridor without being electrocuted by the bare wires dangling in the water.

He really did everything he could for the others before taking his chance. He wanted to put his idea to the test; maybe he was just tired of watching the people he loved die and being unable to save them. He grabs the four corners of the curtain (two corners in each hand) and jumps. At first, the fabric billows like a parachute. His buddies cheer him on. He can see their petrified faces. He picks up speed. His arms have too much weight to carry, the curtain tangles. He's been paragliding in Aspen, so he knows how to use updrafts. Even so, he falls like a stone. I would have liked to be able to say that he made it, but people would simply criticize me for the same reason they criticized Spielberg when he had water gush through the nozzles in the gas chambers. Jeffrey didn't land gracefully on his toes. Within seconds his derisory piece of fabric became a torch. Jeffrey literally exploded on the plaza, killing a firefighter and the woman he was rescuing. Jeffrey's wife got the news of his death from his boyfriend. She found out he was bisexual and that he was dead in the same instant. If I'd hoped to tell charming stories, I picked the wrong subject.

9:36

In a book published in August 2000, I spun a metaphor to describe the entryist revolution: "You can't hijack a plane unless you get on board." Octave Parango was convinced that he could change things from the inside. Then, at the end of the novel, he realized that there was no one to fly the plane. Appointed head of his agency, he discovered it was impossible to revolutionize a system that was autonomous, an organization that had neither manager, nor management, nor purpose. Advertising's capitalist society triumphant and globalized? A rapacious machine running in a vacuum. (The metaphor of a plane without a pilot was borrowed from an American comedy: *Airplane!*) On September 11, 2001, that image appeared to me in all its horrific significance. You have to board a plane in order to hijack it. But what if the plane commits suicide? We become a ball of fire and we're no further on. If we get on board, it is because we want it to change direction, but if it's only to plow it into a building? The only revolution is one external to this self-destructive system. Never board a plane. Accept the world;

participate in advertising or the media and you're certain to die in a colossal explosion live on CNN. Nowadays, entryism has become self-mutilation. The true revolution is effacement. What is important is *not* to play a part. It's time to favor active desertion over passive resistance.

The boycott rather than the sit-in.

Stop blaming others, blaming the world. As the rich man's Zola, it's time for me to write: "*Je m'accuse*"

I accuse myself of complacency and narcissism.

I accuse myself of pathological seduction.

I accuse myself of Park Avenue socialism.

I accuse myself of social climbing and venality.

I accuse myself of jealousy and of frustration.

I accuse myself of affected sincerity.

I accuse myself of trying to please even in this self-accusation intended to parry the blows to come.

I accuse myself of two-speed consciousness.

I accuse myself of appearing on Canal+ to avenge myself for not being a star.

I accuse myself of arrogant indolence.

I accuse myself of writing veiled autobiographies.

I accuse myself of not being the hetero Bruce Benderson.

I accuse myself of being facile at 9:36.

I accuse myself of not being capable of anything much other than facile.

I accuse myself of being entirely responsible for my own depression.

I accuse myself of a complete lack of courage.

I accuse myself of abandoning my child.

I accuse myself of doing nothing to change what is wrong with my life.

I accuse myself of loving all that I disparage, especially money and fame.

I accuse myself of not being able to see further than the end of my twin noses.

I accuse myself of self-satisfaction disguised as self-denigration.

I accuse myself of being incapable of love.

I accuse myself of only seeking the approval of women without ever interesting myself in their problems.

I accuse myself of aesthetics without ethics.

I accuse myself of intellectual (and physical) jerking off.

I accuse myself of mental (and physical) onanism.

I accuse myself of imputing to my generation failings that are mine.

I accuse myself of confusing falling out of love with superficiality (there can be no falling out of love if one is incapable of love).

I accuse myself of looking for the perfect woman knowing that perfection does not exist, doing it so that I will never be happy and can therefore wallow in comfortable whining complaint.

I accuse myself of being uglyist.

I accuse myself of not giving a fuck about anything except myself.

I accuse myself of blaming others because I am jealous of them.

I accuse myself of wanting the best but settling for very little.

I accuse myself of having nothing in common with New York City except perhaps individualism and megalomania.

I accuse myself of burning all my bridges, running from my past, i.e., from myself, and of having no friends.

I accuse myself of vociferous stagnation and clumsy parenting.

I accuse myself of chronic irresponsibility, that is to say ontological cowardice.

I accuse myself of washing my dirty linen in public since 1990.

I accuse myself of leaving nothing in my wake but ruins.

I accuse myself of being infatuated with ruins because "birds of a feather flock together."

And now, the verdict:

I sentence myself to solitary for life.

9:37

THE TRICKY THING IS THERE'S NO PHONE BOOTH AROUND HERE. Clark Kent can't turn into Superman with no phone booth to change into his costume. Dad's hardly gonna get his outfit on in front of Lourdes! Obviously Jerry and me don't care if we see his dick, we've seen it before. But how can he change into a superhero if he can't get dressed? It's silly but I should have thought about it. And Jerry's peed his underwear, dork! Thinks I didn't notice! Is he blind or what? I didn't say anything so as not to distract Dad from his proton metaglucidation. A while back when he went to the bathroom, I thought he was going to transform, but he didn't; I think it's 'cos he doesn't want people to know about his superpowers. It's true, though: superheroes don't usually have kids, so he's gotta keep quiet all the time, it's pretty tough on him. What will he do once he's operational? An excellent question, thank you for asking. Well, he'll start off by melting the steel door with his laser piercing eyes. After that he'll break through to the roof, pick up the whole tower using his ultraforce, and plunge it into the Hudson to put out the flames. It'll go PSCHHHH like when Mom runs water over the pan after she makes popcorn. Then he'll put the tower back where it was and do the same with the tower next door. Or maybe if it's too dangerous and the people inside would get bruises and stuff, he'll do the opposite: he'll suck up 100 billion gallons of water from the sea and spray it all over the Twin Towers. He could do either. Or else, he could make a slide out of plastic sheeting from one of the building sites—there's loads around here—and people can slide down to the bottom, or make a bridge between the towers by stretching his elastic body, or (but he'd only do this as a last resort if the other things didn't work), he could spin the Earth in the opposite direction and make time go backward two hours, that way none of this would have happened and all you need to do is tell the people not to go to work and everything's cool. That's what my dad's gonna do when he gets his trajectorial hyperpowers.

9:38

What most worries the United States is that, on one hand, they control the world; on the other hand, they're no longer in control of anything. I read somewhere that these days David Emil, the owner of Windows on the World, always carries a poem by W. H. Auden everywhere in his wallet:

The winds must come from somewhere when they blow
There must be reasons why the leaves decay
Time can say nothing but I told you so.

Since I arrived in New York, my old reflexes as a society chronicler have taken over: I'm going through *Time Out New York* with a fine-tooth comb, picking up flyers in hip stores, phoning old buddies of mine who are still up for partying, taking notes on the dance floor like I used to when I was twenty and wrote for *Glamour.* . . . Nightlife seems to me a good barometer of how sick or healthy a city is. This one has passed out, stoned on grief and Grey Goose, a new brand of vodka distilled in France. After a string of empty, depressing bars, someone drags me off to Scores, the biggest lap-dancing club in the Big Apple. It's a big, dark space where men, singly or in groups, are prepared to pay twenty bucks, not for the striptease in itself (the girls, who are stunning, strip on stage anyway), but to be tantalized, aroused, bewitched. They pay twenty bucks for the scent of freshly washed hair in their nostrils, the caress of a honeyed knee, the weight of a hand on their shoulder and the burnt caramel flavor of ass against their jeans. People who don't understand lap dancing will never understand America. Here, you pay to get it up without getting it on. You're not buying a girl, but a dream. Eye candy. The United States is the only country where a man is prepared to blow his savings for a whiff of virtuality, to enter an imaginary world. They're not getting a hard-on for nothing, they're doing it for the pleasure of having a hard-on. They're turned on by the unobtainable. It's moralistic (their wives get the benefit when they get home), but above all it's optimistic, ambitious, cerebral: unlike a Frenchman, an American doesn't want to fuck straight off; he prefers the idea of pleasure to pleasure itself, fantasy to reality.

"What are you writing?" Bianca asks, as I jot down this theory in my notebook.

"Nothing, darling."

And she pushes her G-string aside to show me her slit coated with sweet oils. And suddenly I feel very like a typical Frenchman. . . . She breathes into my ear—I can feel her breath—talks to her friend Nikki; how lovely they smell . . . (Chanel No. 5?). Twenty-dollar bills take wing all by themselves in the sweet velvetiness of this convalescent city. Men pay to be frustrated. They believe it is a good thing that not all dreams come true. In America, dreams come true not because Americans want their dreams to come true, but simply because they dream. Dream without thinking of the consequences. For a dream to come true, it must first be dreamed. Run away, girls in Lycra mini-shorts, girls in push-up bras, girls with auburn hair, girls in lace-up boots, girls with polished teeth, girls with oversize breasts, girls who know J. Lo's lyrics by heart ("Don't be fooled by the rocks that I got / I'm still, I'm still Jenny from the block / Used to have a little, now I have a lot / No matter where I go, I know where I came from"), girls in pink high heels, girls with open blouses and black bras, girls showing their bellies, girls with jeweled bellybuttons, girls with tiny flowers tattooed above the cleft of their butts, a sort of profusion, ever-replenished rain of fresh girls, run away! Should you kiss me or give me your number, your empire would crumble

Later, at the Mercer I intend to send out for a call girl (by typing *www.new-york-escorts.com* or *www.manhattangirls.com* into the computer in my room) but I hesitate because the photos can be deceptive: you never know if the girl you'll wind up with will be pretty or ugly. And I'm not drunk enough to fuck ugly. Or too much in love?

9:39

LOURDES JUST GOT A TEXT MESSAGE ON HER PHONE SAYING THE Pentagon has been hit too. This is total war. Where the hell's the army? Is it reassuring to know that we're not the only ones to die? Hell, no. If I knew I was going to buy the farm, I'd have lived my life differently. I'd have fucked bareback. I'd have dumped Mary a lot earlier, traveled a lot more, tried heroin and opium. I'd have spent less time studying and less time working out. I'd have hit on a lot more women instead of hanging back, forever shit-scared of being humiliated. I should have been a gangster, robbed banks, instead of meekly following the law. I should have married Candace so she could be a beautiful widow. I wouldn't have given up smoking. For what? My health? I'd have started a rock band—might as well die of starvation as stick at some pain-in-the-ass job for the money.

I'd have told my boss where to stick his job a lot sooner. I'd have lived in New York, worn a long black coat and sunglasses at night, had a fake tan all year round and had dinner in restaurants where it looks like someone's just turned out the lights, unless maybe there's a power failure—why is it that restaurants are always candlelit in rich countries? Poverty is the luxury of the rich. I'd have bought a lot more cars: what a waste, all that money I'll never spend. I would have tried to have myself cloned. I'd have shaved my head, just to see. I'd have taken more risks since—whatever way you look at it—I've lost.

Or perhaps I should just have been a better man.

9:40

I'D LIKE TO INVENT A NEW GENRE: AUTOSATIRE. I'D LIKE TO KNOW why I've forgotten everything. Why I scribble out my past in my diaries. Why I have to be blind drunk before I can talk to anyone. Why I write rather than create.

I never knew my parents when they were married. I only ever knew them divorced and forced to see each other because of me. Friends, but not lovers. I don't remember ever seeing them kiss other than on the cheek. Is it important? No, because I did the same thing they did. In fact, most people do the same thing: splitting up after the birth of a child has almost become the norm. But if it's so unimportant, why do I feel so choked up talking about it?

A definition of happiness: shrimp fishing at Guéthary. I'm six years old. My grandfather is carrying the butterfly nets (we fish for shrimp with butterfly nets—if Nabokov could see us!). Happiness is the beach at Cenitz at low tide, the rocks pricking your feet, the salt on your back and the sun above. Back then, there was no such thing as an oil slick. They were glorious adventures, except for the shrimp, which ended up being boiled alive in brine. Why is happiness like Guéthary? It must be coincidence that it was at Guéthary that my parents met, fell in love, married.

I feel empty, I want to get smashed, fuck my balls dry, and read books that are not as good as mine. All this to forget that I have no past, that I ring hollow.

When I was five, when my parents were getting divorced, I had nosebleeds so often that the doctors thought I had leukemia. I was happy just to cut class for months on end.

My motto: become what you despise.

Why do we all want to be artists? All the people I meet who are my age write, play, sing, direct, paint, compose. What are they seeking, beauty or truth? It's just a pretext. They want to be famous. We want to be famous because we want to be loved. We want to be loved because we're hurt. We want to mean something. To have purpose. To say something. Not to die anymore. Compensate for the lack of meaning. We want to cease being absurd. Having children is not enough for us. We want to be more interesting than the guy next door. But he wants to be on TV too. That's what's different: our neighbors want to be more interesting than us. Everyone is jealous of everyone else now that Art is completely narcissistic.

In Times Square they've just opened a huge Toys R Us, even more enormous than the great toy store FAO Schwarz. I ride the escalators of the megastore, a five-floor building bursting with toys, Muzak, garish colors, merchandising spinoffs. I'm attacked from all sides by giant robots, tame tyrannosauruses, Playstations 2, 3, 8, 47. . . . Why do I find these places so appallingly depressing? Toys have become one of America's most important industries. Every day a new Disney megastore or a new Toys R Us opens. Here, parents spend more and more money to assuage their guilt. Megastores make it possible for kids to escape their parents, and vice versa.

9:41

"DAD, YOU MEAN YOU'RE NOT A SUPERHERO?"

It was 9:41 when David, who had never cried in his life, started to cry. Oh, not all of a sudden, no; it took him some time to realize what was happening to him. The corners of his mouth dropped, making a circumflex, like Charlie Brown in the funnies. His eyes widened to three times their normal size. He stared at the securely sealed door, the broken lock, the worthless handle, the red plastic sign on which was written the barefaced lie: EMERGENCY EXIT. Suddenly, his bottom lip swelled, reaching up toward his little nose, and his chin began to quiver uncertainly. Jerry and I looked at each other, speechless: what did this new expression mean? It was hardly the moment to be trying out new faces on his poor family. David rubbed his hair, unsure of what was happening to him. We could hear his breathing get faster. I thought he was suffocating again, though there was less smoke than there had been earlier. His breathing became labored, as if an alien buried inside him for eons was trying to find a way out. David the dispassionate, David who was toughness incarnate, David the phlegmatic was dissolving into tears for the first time. His mouth opened wide to let out a great howl of rage. He stuttered frantic syllables: "But, but, why, but, it's, we, but, what . . ."—which, added together, ended up as one long "WAAAAAA," which set off the sprinklers in his eyes, the heavy tears rolling down his pink cheeks. Jerry stared hard at me so as not to cry too, but since I burst into tears, he broke down too. We hugged each other hard, like a football team at half time—except we weren't wearing helmets, and we were crying because we'd lost the game.

I used to think that having kids was the best way of triumphing over death. Even that's not true. It is possible to die with them, and it is as though we had never existed.

9:42

DIFFICULT TO IMAGINE A MORE FRAGILE CITY. SUCH AN INTENSE concentration of people in such a small area makes an attractive target for destroyers of all sorts. If you want to cause maximum damage for minimum effort, New York seems an ideal target. And New Yorkers know this now: towers are vulnerable, the whole city is potentially a heap of scrap iron, a monument in crystal. Never in the history of humanity has such a commanding location been so easy to obliterate. And yet intelligent people still live there. It's like San Francisco: they know that one day a horrific earthquake will plunge the city into the ocean, but they don't run away. This is another admirable American phenomenon: New York and San Francisco are both megalopolises with apocalyptic destinies, but no one thinks to desert them. A New Yorker's personality is forged by this contradiction: the awareness of the threat in no way slows the frenzied pace of life; on the contrary, it provides the fuel.

Amnesiac memories of the American nights of my childhood . . . Ronald Reagan was president. . . . Every night we had the choice . . . the five-floor Danceteria . . . the Palladium, where the john was decorated by the latest graffiti artists . . . Webster Hall, with its interminable line . . . Area, which was redecorated every month, with actors in glass cages . . . Nell's, which looked like a huge private apartment . . . the neo-gothic cathedral that was the Limelight . . . Club USA. . . . How many countries do you know where a nightclub is named after the country itself? All these nebulous places, long since disappeared into the mists of the past, the amnesia of far-off parties. . . . And now, nothing . . . lounges with subdued lighting . . . meager customers . . . microscopic clubs that are empty all the same . . . sleek restaurants . . . candlelit cellars . . . bygone magic.

9:42 P.M. I'm visiting a great French writer, now eighty years old, in an apartment laid on him by New York University. His wife tells me that all the S&M clubs have closed: the Vault, Hellfire, La Nouvelle Justine no longer exist. Tonight, she's going to a "submit party," but she can't take me because it's a women-only night. I've brought a bottle of Francis Ford Coppola's California red, but the great writer does not open it, preferring to offer me a glass of sherry that tastes like maple syrup. It's like drinking pancakes; it's exquisite. I feel infinitely comfortable with this free, happy couple, married since 1957. The great writer tells me about his meeting with William Burroughs in La Coupole. A sinister guy, like all addicts.

"He killed his wife," he says, looking over at his own. "But he took her to Mexico to do it."

"If you ever take me to Mexico, I'll be on my guard," she retorts, smiling.

I tell them there's a new bar in Soho called Naked Lunch. The great writer jokes: "And is one obliged to lunch in the nude?"

His latest novel has just been translated here, under the title *Repetition*. Then the great writer informs me that I am to be published in the United States and that we are shortly going to dine with his friend Edmund White to celebrate the fact. There is a rapprochement between my origins and myself. I am returning to my grandmother's country. I have not managed to rid myself of my roots, my history, my blood. Not such a man of the world as all that, anchored in spite of myself.

"Why come to New York to write about it?" the great writer asks, stroking his white beard. "I'm writing a novel set in Berlin, I'm not going to Berlin to write it."

"Well, I'm writing an *ancien roman*. I leave the *nouveau* to young men like you!"

A little later, in Thom's Bar, warmed by the fire in the hearth and a frozen margarita, I consider asking my fiancée to marry me. You see, I'd like us to be free and beautiful for fifty years like the Robbe-Grillets.

9:43

THE LIGHTS GO OUT, COME ON AGAIN. THE BULBS START TO FLICKER like strobe lights in a disco. Then, it's black as night. The kids scream inconsolably in the darkness. We are in the depths of hell. I have no choice anymore. Either we wait to die here or we go back down to the restaurant. I don't hesitate for long, it's too awful to stay put.

"Come on sweethearts, we're going back downstairs."

They cry even harder. I grip their hands tightly and we stand up. Lourdes shakes her head, she prefers to stay here. We hug her for a long moment. She takes off her Windows on the World lapel badge and proffers it like a relic.

"See you; if not here, then somewhere . . ."

"Bless you, Carthew. With your two little angels beside you."

"You sure you don't want to come back down?"

"Pray for me. When they come and open the door I'll come get you. Go on, now, git!"

And we leave her, sitting in the dark, beautiful as the world.

* * *

Passing the offices of Windows, I find an iBook hooked up to the Internet. I make the most of it to write an e-mail to Candace as fast as I can without rereading or correcting the typos. “Canda, you cheated on me because you thought I wasn’t serious. So what? It’s not importnat you body doesn’t beloing to me. The only thing that belongs to us is our loneliness, and you interrupted mine with your cheeerfullness, your pink lips, your sadness, your shaved vagina. I was scarend to say ‘I love you’. But I wasd a poor schumk not to take you seroiusly. I’ve found my only memeories are of you. Candae, try to forgibve me. I am going to die here, I’m gettng weaker every minute and you can save me, when I rememerber us, I can see that I was trying to eb someone else, I was playing a part, I don’t know what I wanted frmom you, for you to touch me, but you aved me, you came into my life to late, I’d already done everything, I didn’t give you the space you deserved, I don’t know where to start, but I’ve gotan excuse it’s because I was dying, Don’t forget your Carthe.” Okay, that’s what I should have liked to write if I’d had the time. The e-mail she received was shorter: “I loved U. C.Y.”

I step over an upended pile of CD-Rs. A shelf has collapsed and the office craft knives are scattered over the linoleum.

9:44

I am dazzled by the glorious collapse of the world.

—Henry Miller
Black Spring

I'M GOING MAD: I COLLECT EVERY NEWSPAPER CLIPPING WITH MY name on it. I cut them out and file them away so I can show them to my daughter twenty years from now when I'm a has-been:

"See, honey? Daddy was really famous when he was young. It's a pity you didn't see that! People loved me, I swear, ask your mother, it was out of control, that's why she kicked me out!"

"Yeah, sure, you were a star, Dad. . . . You've shown me this file, like, four times. . . . And don't bullshit: I know why Mom kicked you out, and it had nothing to do with that. You were just impossible to live with."

"But, you . . . you do love me?"

At this point, I prefer not to imagine what my daughter's response will be twenty years from now.

After their success, some people do a disappearing act; I decided to go for omnipresence, overexposure. I don't see why I should disappear because people like me. I prefer to wait until everyone's well and truly sick of me before disappearing for good. The time is coming.

In my paranoid fantasies, it seems to me the system has been rigged to trivialize my revolution, that giving me money, success, fame, recognition is designed to make my pseudo-revolution look obtuse. I am not yet sure whether this lavish punishment will work. Is it possible to be muzzled by luxury? Can success be the spectacular funeral cortège of revolution? That's certainly the method Enver Hoxha opted for in making Ismail Kadaré deputy. It is based on invalidating the writer's grievance by making him powerful. How can anyone believe in what Americans call the "limousine liberal," what we in France refer to as the "Gauche caviar"? Is it possible to be rich but sympathetic to change? Yes: you need only cultivate ingratitude. To be a "BoBo" or a "RiRe" simply means you haven't outgrown ingratitude. Being a "bourgeois bohemian" is a good thing, much better than being a bourgeois period. I'm sick and tired of people saying I'm just a spoiled brat smashing his toys. I'm smashing them so I can create others.

9:45

My ancestor, John Adams, signed a treaty with Libya in Tripoli on June 10, 1797, indicating to the Ottoman Empire (which at the time ruled the Maghreb) that America was "in no way founded on the Christian faith." There is no American crusade against Islam! The first war in Afghanistan was against the Russians, not the Afghanis.

Later an alliance grew up between born-again Christians and Saudi Wahhabis (disciples of Mohammed Ibn Abdulwahhab, 1703–1792, the "Calvin of the Sands"). We often forget that Islam, like Judeo-Christian faiths, claims its descent from Abraham. The religion in power in America is a sister-enemy of the fundamentalist Islam. We are witnessing a new Saint Bartholomew; Jerry and David are the victims of a Saint Bartholomew's Day massacre perpetrated by the oil-producing nations. Christian fundamentalists face down Muslim fundamentalists: I am going to die because of an incestuous quarrel between billionaire sects.

But I never believed in it! My parents campaigned against abortion, against alcohol, against prostitution and homosexuality, but Mom was on the pill, Dad drank every night, and whores and faggots overran Texas like they did the rest of the country! I never approved of their education; at college, I even campaigned briefly for the Communist Party USA, just to piss off my Dad, who supported Reagan! Why should I have to pay for them? Take my parents; they've had their time, them and their "compassionate conservatism"! I was a fucking Marxist, not an evangelist! Oh God, I'm losing it . . .

"Dad, I've got a headache . . ."

"Breathe through your mouth."

We descend into the black cloud of Windows on the World.

9:46

NEW YORK IS A BOUDOIR WHERE THEY SERVE YOU SALMON MOUSSE everywhere, or salmon en croûte, or just plain salmon. What is it with Americans and salmon? That's all they eat. In Paris it's "salad of young green seasonal shoots," here it's salmon steak, salmon tartare. Paradoxically, the hip neighborhood is the Meatpacking District.

The clubs in the Meatpacking District are faithful to the name of the neighborhood: they really are meat markets. Models dance like hunks of meat hanging from hooks. I ask some New Yorker coked up to the eyeballs where he goes to chill out away from the city of lunatics. Ibiza, he says. Some New Yorkers are absolutely incorrigible. No one can save them from their apocalypse. The beauty of fury.

The bouncer at Cielo doesn't seem too open-minded.

"Are you on the list?"

"Um . . . yeah, sure . . ."

"Your name, sir?"

"My name is Osama, Osama Bin fucking Laden, OK?"

You have to be able to run fast after making a terrible joke in front of a bouncer.

It's a rare thing, a writer afraid of the book he's writing.

At the Taj, I admire a tall, sad, long-haired blonde dressed in black, surrounded by brothers. I don't remember how I get talking to her. Maybe I spill my drink over her, jostled by some stoned French kid. I apologize and wipe my apple martini over her pale breasts. That's when she says her bodyguards are going to break my face. I ask her to reason with them. She laughs, introduces me to her two giant brothers. I comment that her nail polish is the same color as her bubblegum. I ask her where she's going later. When you're anonymous in a distant city, you might as well exploit the situation and be direct. She says they're going to Lotus. Then she disappears into the crowd. I take a taxi to go wait for her at Lotus. An hour later, I'm wasted by the time she arrives accompanied by her henchmen. She smiles when she recognizes me. To keep an American woman happy, you have to give her tokens of persistence. Her every gesture is beautiful. She looks touched by my presence, embarrassed by her overprotective brothers. She comes over to talk to me, touches my arm. I tell her I've always dreamed of having kids with a model. She asks if I'm French. I put on my Spanish accent. Her laugh is like crystal. I pour her a drink, which she downs in one gulp. New York women are crystalline but tough. It is she who leans toward my mouth. She kisses me; her tongue is cold and wet from the ice. Her neck smells of soap. I was wondering whether my pecker was up to functioning tonight, but it's fine—I get a hard-on straight off. I ask her name. Candace, she says. I ask her what she does for a living. Victoria's Secret catalogs, she tells me. She asks what I do for a living. New York women often ask this question, then mentally calculate your salary. I tell her I'm writing a novel about Windows on the World. Her face becomes blank. It's as though I'd hit her with a baseball bat. She tells me she has to get back to her little group, that she'll be right back. She never returns.

9:47

A hundred times I have thought: New York is a catastrophe,
And fifty times: It is a beautiful catastrophe.

—Le Corbusier

DID YOU KNOW THAT THERE WERE TWO TOWERS OF BABEL? Archaeologists are categorical. The ruins of a ziggurat still stand today in Borsippa, on the banks of the Euphrates, a few miles south of Babylon—an edifice that local tradition, both Christian and Muslim, claims is the tower of Babel (the House of the Seven Guides of Heaven and Earth). The ruins rise up to 155 feet, with a section of wall at the summit. Local legend has it that a comet, sent by God to punish the blasphemers, smashed into the tip, causing a fire the evidence for which is still borne by the blackened bricks (you can check on site).

But there was a second tower, a little to the north. Rebuilt in Babylon, the second Tower of Babel has been gradually destroyed by centuries of invasions. Today, all that remains are sections of the foundations, but according to Herodotus (fifth century B.C.), who claimed to have climbed the steps, it was 299 feet high and was made up of seven levels.

There were once Twin Towers of Babel . . . in Iraq.

9:48

ART SPIEGELMAN SAID IT BEST: HE SAID NEW YORKERS TURNED toward the World Trade Center as though toward Mecca. Did the towers fulfill some spiritual emptiness? They were the legs that supported the American dream. It's difficult to imagine what the World Trade Center looked like at dusk: two columns of light, and—seen close up—thousands of tiny yellow squares, the lighted windows of little offices, a giant chessboard of polished glass in which thousands of marionettes answered their phones, typed into their word processors, came and went, a cup of decaf always in hand, flourished important pieces of paper, sent urgent e-mails to the whole world, these thousands of flames in the twilight, this luminous anthill, this atomic reactor from which everything departed, to which everything arrived, the indomitable lighthouse of the world, this sword piercing the clouds of the dying day, which served as a sign to New Yorkers when the sky veered to red and they felt their souls fade.

9:49

In the Windows, the few remaining survivors intone Irving Berlin's "God Bless America" (1939).

9:50

SOMETHING ELSE HAS CHANGED SINCE THE EIGHTIES: BACK THEN, New Yorkers said "Hi"; now, they say, "Hey, what's up?" The way they say hello is less subtle, more surprised. I remember "Hi" as a greeting that was smiling, polite, happy to see you. "Hey" sounds different since the tragedy. I hear it as a "hey, what are you doing here? Good for you, you're still alive." But it's probably just my paranoia again. I circle the building like a vulture in search of corpses. I wander the vertical streets breathing in fresh calamity. A writer is a jackal, a coyote, a hyena. Give me my dose of desolation. I'm looking for a tragedy; don't suppose you've got some little atrocity on hand? I chew on Bubble Yum and the heartache of orphans.

Some critics claim cinema is a "window on the world." Others say the novel is. Art is a window on the world. Like the tinted windows of the glass towers, in which I can see my reflection, a tall, stooped silhouette in a black coat, a heron with glasses walking with enormous strides. Fleeing the image, I walk faster, but it follows me like a bird of prey. Writing an autobiographical novel not to reveal oneself, but to melt away. A novel is a two-way mirror behind which I hide so I can see and not be seen. The mirror in which I see myself, in the end, I give to others.

When one cannot answer the question "Why?" one must at least attempt to answer the question "How?"

Grief does not prevent wealthy old women from walking their dogs on Madison Avenue nor street hawkers from displaying their fake Gucci bags on the sidewalk a block from the real Gucci store. There are gallery openings still where everyone dresses in black; there are clubs still where you *have* to be on the guest list; there are hotels still where everything—from the guests to the decor—is beautiful. At 9:50, in a further attempt to go back in time, I step into 95 Wall Street, the building where I worked during the eighties, to see whether it will trigger some Proustian memory within me. There is still a CRÉDIT LYONNAIS logo on the lobby wall, but the receptionist explains that the French bank moved up to midtown some time ago. How do you go from Proust to Modiano in ten seconds? The deserted lobby. The doorman's suspicious look. The tight-lipped security guards. The mysterious businessmen. The hazy memory. Did I really spend every day here? There's no point hanging around, nothing is coming back to me.

"Sir, you can't stay here."

The stocky uniformed guy comes over to me slowly.

"But I worked here a long time ago . . ."

I put on my Spanish accent, but there's nothing doing. I'm evicted by my past. My past wants nothing to do with me. My past accompanies me through the revolving door. I'm forced to turn my back on it once again.

9:51

WILD TRADE CENTER

CAT STEVENS SANG "OOH, BABY, BABY, IT'S A WILD WORLD." I USED to have all his records. Cat Stevens was one of my idols along with Neil Young and James Taylor. So many moving songs, so many extraordinary miniatures, delicate crystalline. The music of *Harold and Maude*. Uncompromising lyrics over heartbreaking melodies, lyrical but simple. As if this singer/songwriter had been touched by something greater than him, as though he had access to some higher power. "When I'm alone," he said, "the songs just come."

Time leaves you nothing
Nothing at all
("Time," 1970)

Oh mama, mama see me, . . . I'm a pop star [. . .]
Oh mama, mama see me . . . on the TV
("Pop Star," 1970)

Trouble, oh, trouble set me free
("Trouble," 1970)

Cat Stevens's great theme is the loss of innocence. The beginning of "Where Do the Children Play?" resonates oddly at 9:51:

Well I think it's fine, building jumbo planes [. . .]
Will you tell us when to live,
will you tell us when to die?

I could play the game of terrible omens by quoting "Morning Has Broken," "Home in the Sky," and also an earlier song, "The View from the Top" (1967): "*The view from the top can be oh so very lonely*."

Cat Stevens had the simplicity of the true poet, but to me he was more than that. He was my brother in loneliness, my friend, my fellow traveler. I would hang out in my bedroom in Texas for hours, barefoot on my bed, looking at the album covers. His acoustic guitar gave me a feeling of peace. Back then, album covers were twelve inches. When CDs replaced records, music became "the record industry." The change sent out a message: music is no longer a thing of contemplation but of consumption in its plastic packaging. I could talk to you for hours about the crying trashcan. On the album cover of *Mona Bone Jakon,* there's a gray trashcan crying a single tear. Can you think of a better metaphor for our times? We've created a world of crying garbage cans. I love the strange titles, too—*Tea for the Tillerman, Teaser and the Firecat*—and the overblown Elton John–style covers. And the lavish arrangements (*Rolling Stone* called them "lush"). The violins on "Lily-white" (1970): the finest bridge in pop music since Ben E. King's "Stand By Me."

Cat Stevens tried to say something, then he disappeared.

You will still be here tomorrow
But your dreams may not
("Father and Son," 1970)

He wrote all these masterpieces in the same year—between January and July 1970—at the age of twenty-two, while in the hospital recovering from an almost fatal bout of tuberculosis. The romantics' disease: a bad cough left untreated made worse through an excess of drugs, alcohol, women, and sleepless nights. It was in the hospital that Cat Stevens let his beard grow.

On December 23, 1977, having sold 40 million copies of his albums—seven of which were in the Top 10 albums throughout the seventies—Cat Stevens disappeared. The star of the swinging sixties, the shy guy who had groupies screaming his name the moment he stepped out of his Rolls-Royce, who was permanently recording or touring, lived the rock star life, drugs and sex in luxury hotels, the only Englishman since the Beatles and the Stones to have become a star in America, the man who sold out Madison Square Garden two nights running (the audience gave standing ovations in the middle of the songs), Cat Stevens turned toward Islam in 1977. It was his brother who offered him the Koran. He visited a mosque in Jerusalem. On July 4, 1978, he changed his name to Yusuf Islam. He was thirty-one. No star of his magnitude had ever given up everything so abruptly. He auctioned his white piano and his gold discs and distributed the money among various charities. He announced that he would never again write except to communicate the word of Muhammad. When Salman Rushdie was condemned to death by the Ayatollah Khomeini, Yusuf Islam declared on British television that "the punishment for blasphemy is death." This is the same man who wrote "Peace Train." He wears a turban, has a long beard, babouches, and traditional Arab dress. He funds a Koranic school which he set up on the outskirts of London. He considers himself to have been "saved by Islam."

I should have converted to Islam too, like Cat Stevens and Cassius Clay. I would have left Carthew Yorston behind. I would have adopted an Arabic name: Shafeeq Abdullah. I would have renamed Jerry and David: Mohammed and Ali. I would have stopped eating bacon.

Ooh, baby, baby, it's a wild world.

I make this solemn oath
If we make it out of here
I'll convert us to Islam.

9:52

I REMEMBER FRAGMENTS OF AMERICA. WHEN I WAS TEN YEARS OLD, I filmed the World Trade Center. My father had given me a Super-8 camera. We'd taken a taxi to the two towers. The buildings were like a corridor; it was like shooting rapids at the bottom of a canyon. I wasn't in a city, I was at the bottom of a chasm. Buildings reflected the buildings opposite. I was minuscule but multiplied like in the maze of mirrors at the Jardin d'Acclimatation. When we arrived on the forecourt, my first action as a director was to take a low angle shot of one of the towers. Seen from below, the tower looked like a highway to heaven. The grooves were the white lines that cars would get fined for crossing. I couldn't film for very long; Super-8 films lasted only three minutes. It was important not to make mistakes since you couldn't record over them: the mistake was indelible. I probably did a sequence shot of One World Trade Center, then Two, then back to One. My dumb low-angle shot made me dizzy, I was leaning back so far, I nearly broke my neck. It was the first time I realized that being on the ground looking up was as frightening as being high up looking down.

The crushing size of these colossuses was my first contact with the metaphysical—catechism lessons at the École Bossuet were less exotic. I not only felt stunned, I felt *physically dominated* by these concrete monsters. Something existed that was more powerful than us. The energy that had inspired these buildings was not human. Even so, the space between the pillars had been calculated by the architect to precisely equal the span of my father's shoulders. Despite the immensity of the towers, there was something organic about them. This something, which was more powerful than us, was us all the same. The warm summer wind whirled about on the plaza, carrying the greasy smell of hot dogs with sweet mustard. I whirled too; I filmed the tourists walking across the granite flagstones, my brother Charles, a couple of kids roller-skating, a dancer moving like a robot. But I kept coming back to the two towers; my camera was literally drawn toward these two pillars of the firmament. Above our heads, the two towers seemed to merge, welded together like a triumphal arch, an upturned V. Only a timid band of sky regretfully separated them. To build such a monstrosity you had to be mad or have the soul of a child, or both. I was astonished at the passersby who went about their business without realizing that they were weaving beneath a giant's legs. Above their heads, they had balanced a dangerous whim.

9:53

It would have been better all around to leave Manhattan to the Indians. The mistake dates from 1626, when Peter Minuit threw his 24 dollars down the drain. Should have been suspicious of someone with a name like Peter Midnight: midnight is the witching hour. Peter Minuit was proud as punch to have swindled the Algonquins, palming them off with a few glass beads in exchange for their island. But it was the Indians who swindled the palefaces. The glass beads were seeds that, planted in the earth, grew into a city of glass less substantial than a teepee.

9:54

I'm bored with writing dead-end novels. Bored with sterile post-existentialist meanderings. Tired of being a catcher in the rye catching nothing. I need to find the new utopia.

It seems increasingly clear to me that the terrorists were mistaken in their target. Why didn't they attack the United Nations buildings on First Avenue between 42nd and 46th streets? Because it's an international zone? But the organization has clearly failed in its mission. The UN is really to blame for wars, injustice, and inequality. It allows nations to believe that justice exists when it's never enforced. Target your Boeings on that thingamajig. The world needs an effective government, an international army capable of imposing order. The blue berets in Yugoslavia? Nothing more than unarmed soldiers paid to watch massacres without turning a hair. The United Nations was discredited the moment it appointed Libya president of the Commission for Human Rights. This bureaucratic, sclerotic, corrupt, and impotent organization needs to be reformed. The UN was founded on the ruins of the League of Nations; what are we going to build on the ruins of the UN? Why not global democracy of the type called for in the speeches of Garry Davis, founder of the World Citizens Movement in 1948 (with the support of Albert Camus, André Breton, and Albert Einstein)? There is a solution to the horrors of terrorism and ecological catastrophe: a global republic governed by an international parliament elected by universal suffrage. I dream of abolishing nations. I would love not to have a country. John Lennon droned, "Imagine there's no countries." Could this be why New York assassinated him?

In the UN sculpture garden, I take a photo of a statue of St. George slaying a dragon that looks uncannily like the fuselage of an airplane. Numerous TV broadcast trucks outside make it difficult to see. Entitled "Good Defeats Evil," this massive sculpture was a gift to the United Nations from the USSR in 1990. It is sculpted from the remains of two missiles, one Soviet, one American. "Good Defeats Evil": it is a battle that rages in each of us every day and presently throughout the world. In this square building, the members of the Security Council are gathered to vote on a resolution about the war in Iraq. At a press conference last night, President Bush said something rather fine: "Since September eleventh . . . our country is a battlefield."

The weird melting pot that works in New York should serve as an example: a world without frontiers must be possible, since it's been tried and tested successfully on this tiny island. The results are dirty, complicated, dangerous, and noisy, but the system works: it is possible to live with people of all

Good Defeats Evil

races and origins, from all over the world: it's feasible, it can be done. Look at Sarajevo.

I've met Troy Davis a number of times in Paris. My first impression was of a tall, lanky man exhausted by the mission conferred on him by his father. Nevertheless, he seems very methodical: he lugs his briefcase around countless countries. The first time I met him, he was looking for money from Pierre Bergé, the French entrepreneur. I found him less entertaining the second time, since he was looking for money from me. Troy Davis is permanently broke: he spends all his money on airline tickets since he quit his job to dedicate himself to the cause of world democracy. He had a plan for a "Protest for World Democracy." I remember putting him in touch with writer Jean-

Paul Enthoven, mostly in an attempt to be rid of him. After that, we communicated mostly by e-mail. He wanted to hit my brother up for money; he bugged me until I gave him Ardisson's cell number. . . . As soon as he found out I was going to be a publisher, he returned to the fray with his book project. To be honest, he was starting to get on my tits, him and his World Democracy. Even so, though I racked my brains I couldn't think of any other post–September 11 utopia.

9:55

INTERNET DATING WILL SOON HAVE A NEW TWIST. SOON YOU'LL BE able to upload a mini-bio filmed with a webcam spelling out exactly what you're looking for in a person: age, location, hobbies, eye color, etc. Soon, you won't meet anyone by accident anymore. You'll introduce yourself on the Internet with a photo or a video and say "I'm looking for a sex-obsessed bisexual redhead with big tits and a tight pussy into partner-swapping, Cat Stevens records, basketball, Tarantino movies, and the Republican Party." You'll receive an e-mail or IM alert when someone matching your criteria is in your neighborhood. No need to go to dumbass bars anymore. It's a pity I won't live to see this brave new world where dating is as logical as real-estate advertising. I wanted to live in a virtual world; I'm dying in a real one.

9:56

HERE ON THE BROOKLYN BRIDGE, I FEEL AS THOUGH I'M STANDING on the edge of a cliff. I marvel at the East River, at the tugboats that whistle and inscribe white crested waves on the sea. The white lines of boats on the sea mirror the white lines of planes in the sky. Since I stopped taking cocaine, I see white lines everywhere. Are there powdered humans still in the New York air? Everyone living in the city knows that he must have breathed them into his lungs. In my first novel, Octave snorts his boss's ashes. To a greater or lesser extent, New Yorkers too have done this: become involuntary cannibals, contaminated by a form of anthrax containing high-grade volatile humanity. There were outbreaks of illness in Lower Manhattan and Brooklyn (everywhere the cloud of smoke passed). The government apparently decided to play down the health risks so as not to further panic the populace.

A photographer on board stated: "We made a number of passes over the roofs to see whether anyone had managed to get up there. There was no one. Given the situation, what could we have done? It would have been dangerous to land, especially as the smoke made any kind of maneuvering risky. What we should probably have done was let down a rope. Sadly, I was pretty sure that the doors to the roof would be locked for security reasons. The heat was horrendous. We could feel it from the cockpit, and the pilot could read it on the external thermometer. We couldn't see anything inside the towers, but I could see people leaning out of the shattered windows, some of them covered in blood, their clothes ripped or burned. Some of them signaled to us, but what could we do? I often remember one woman: she was hanging on with one hand and waving to us with the other. . . . But what could we do?"

"What could we do?" is a question he will probably ask himself until his dying day. What could they do? The advantage of writing this much later, a Parisian tourist writing from the comfort of my armchair, is that I can answer without panicking, without risking my neck. What they should have done was contact the Security Staff and get them to open the doors to the roof, or get a message to the firefighters in the building who were on the 22nd floor, then organize a series of helicopter airlifts like they do with rescues at sea or in the mountains. It should have been fairly routine, given the dangers helicopter pilots face rescuing people from avalanches or hurricanes. In my mind I have a recurring image that I find deeply moving: a helicopter winching people clinging to a rope ladder to safety above the World Trade Center. The image would have been the most beautiful response to the suicide planes. Unfortunately, it's an image we never got to see.

9:57

I HAD A BAD IDEA, THOUGH BORN OF THE BEST OF INTENTIONS: I offered the kids the Windows on the World lapel badge that Lourdes gave me when she said goodbye. The problem is that she only had one. Jerry and David started squabbling over who should get it. In the end, Jerry got to keep it, because physically he's the stronger of the two. I didn't have the heart to impose some alternative justice. David sulked, but strangely, the quarrel changed his mood, and to my great relief he stopped crying. He was plotting his revenge. A couple of seconds later as Jerry was pinning the thing on his T-shirt, David elbowed him so that he'd prick himself with the pin. There was a drop of blood. Jerry gritted his teeth, David smiled. An eye for an eye, a tooth for a tooth. Jerry accepted it: that was life. I tousled his hair: I had just worked out the problem with this planet. There weren't enough lapel badges for everyone.

9:58

IN THE END, I TRACKED DOWN TROY DAVIS, WITH HIS GRAY TWEED suit, his gray coat, and his gray briefcase. Like all utopians, Troy doesn't care about fashion, since he lives in the future, decades from now. Lenin looked like an accountant too, eating complimentary bread at La Closerie des Lilas. We're sitting in the Life Café with some sandwiches, the floor is tiled, the clientele studenty, clusters of cheerful girls and slightly kitsch paintings on the walls. Troy is two years older than me. He went to Harvard, like my father, though he studied physics.

"I'm shattered, but at least we're getting somewhere: the action committee for the World Parliament has the support of Edgar Morin, Jacques Delors, Sonia Gandhi, Felipe González, Nelson Mandela, Shimon Peres, Danièle Mitterrand, Javier Pérez de Cuéllar, Leah Rabin, Michel Rocard, Raymond Barre, Amartya Sen [winner of the Nobel Prize for Economics 1998], Alejandro Toledo [president of Peru], Marceau the mime, l'Abbé Pierre . . ."

"Very classy. Sounds like the guest list for a drinks party at Jacques Chirac's."

"Yeah. Maybe you want to be on the committee just to get an invite?"

"I don't need to do that to get an invite. All I have to do is publish some bestsellers. In concrete terms, can you explain to me how setting up new institutions will speed up the implementation of the Tobin tax, or wipe out third world debt, for example?"

"A new, democratic world order would have the political clout to enact those kinds of laws. To set up a tax on carbon emissions, regulate arms sales, or set up a global environmental agency. The problem of our times is that we have a globalized economy but no globalized government. There has to be a revolution in order to enact new laws. People have forgotten that the revolutions of 1776 and 1789 were the basis for the subsequent financial revolution."

"You really think you'll see something like this in your lifetime?"

"History makes intermittent leaps (the most recent example being the collapse of communism). And then there's the ICC [International Criminal Court]: that's the first time world citizenship has been legally recognized. With an intelligent public awareness campaign, we could create a World Parliament within ten years."

"And where do you set it up, this parliament? In the States, like the UN?"

"No, on a man-made island that is constantly moving between the five continents. A massive project for the shipyards of the world."

"You know what I like about you? You're mad. What about a novel? Do you think a novel could help?"

"Sure—unless you're the author! Hundreds of thousands of

young people already demonstrate out of sheer idealism, though no one has put forward a coherent plan. When they find out about this plan for peace and unity, there'll be millions of them. The world protest against the war in Iraq on February 15, 2003, rallied 15 million people on the planet. February 15 is a date which is just as important as September 11: the first worldwide protest march. The global demo!"

"You don't think it's too late, that we're already living through the apocalypse, that cynicism will always triumph over utopianism? That we should just leave Jimmy Carter to worry about world peace?"

"Whichever way you look at it, even from a cynical point of view, we have to find some non-totalitarian way of solving the problems of globalization. The problem of world hunger could be resolved in less than five years, but it isn't, because there are too many conflicting interests getting in the way. Then we'll come to the wars over water. Decisions have to be taken by the people of earth as a whole, not just a handful of politicians in the pay of water and power companies. If not, then we should tell it like it is: we're living under the yoke of a global dictatorship."

"'Global dictatorship'? Listen to you! People are free, in rich countries at least."

"It's not my phrase, it's from Camus."

"Oh, right, well, if it's Camus that changes everything. OK, Remind me to take you to 56 rue Jacob next time you're in Paris. That's where it all started, the birth of a nation, as Griffith used to say."

"Please! Don't bullshit with your mouth full. It started a long time before that—you have to go back to the Sumerians.

Until 5000 B.C. we lived in paradise. There were no states. It was a bunch of Sumerian kings who invented war and absolutist nationalism. And you know where it happened? In Iraq! Since the Kingdom of Sumer, it's been war. Right now, in his dealings with Saddam Hussein, Bush is behaving like a petty Mesopotamian kinglet."

"Don't be too hard on the Sumerians. They invented writing, too. Without the Sumerians, I'd have to be a TV presenter."

The Life Café is aptly named, full of highbrow claptrap that makes you want to change the world, and girls called Sandy with squeaky-clean hair.

"Tell me, Troy, what are you going to call this idea of yours? You know you've got to have an 'ism,' otherwise no one will take your utopia seriously. I suggest 'alt-globalism' to contrast with globalization, or maybe 'Internationalism.' Except that sounds too commie . . . 'Multilateralism'? 'Cosmopolitanism'? 'Globalism'? No, sounds too capitalist."

"Well, I hadn't really thought about it, but it seems to me it's pretty incidental . . ."

"Oh, no! Not at all. It's very important to have a name that makes people want to get involved. 'Universalism'? No, sounds too much like Vivendi. I've got it: 'Planetarism.' There you go. We're planetarists."

"Sounds like some suicidal sect."

"Too bad. You're the Charles Fourier of the new century. You're our non-Raelian guru. Oh, Saint Troy, show us the way!"

"Frédéric?"

"Yes?"

"How many caipirinhas have you had?"

"Oh, shut up. I suppose you think Karl Marx drank mineral water?"

We were talking nonsense, just bullshitting; all the same, it felt good to believe in something.

9:59

ANOTHER TREMOR.

"What the hell was that?"

"The other tower has just collapsed," says someone who has been leaning out to breathe.

The cloud is so thick it's impossible to tell smoke from dust. The tower that was struck after ours collapsed first. Not trying to figure out but figuring out all the same: that means our tower will implode in a few minutes.

"Let us pray. Lord God, I pray to You even though I don't believe in You. Bring us unto You, in spite of our opportunism."

The collapse of the other tower made the sound of a handful of broken spaghetti strands, nothing more. I suppose it's the same sound an avalanche makes. A sharp snap. Mass murder doesn't rumble like thunder; mass murder makes the sound of a cookie being crunched. Or Niagara Falls, if you replace the water with concrete.

At some point, Jerry looked round at the water cooler, which was making a strange glug-glug noise. Bubbles were starting to form in the clear plastic water bottle. Inside, the water was about to boil.

10:00

LOWER MANHATTAN WITHOUT THE TWO TOWERS IS A DIFFERENT city: twenty-eight years have gone up in smoke. It was at these docks that Lafayette put ashore.

Lower Manhattan is the only part of the city where the streets don't have numbers, the only part where one can get lost, retrace one's steps; the Financial District is the one which most resembles the jumble of a European city. At ten o'clock in the morning, I walk down Wall Street, the street of the wall of money—so named because this was where they built the ramparts to protect the city from the Indians. Now, someone needs to add another brick to the wall, as in the Pink Floyd song. In Israel, they're building a wall like the one in Berlin. Soon, it won't be Wall Street, but "Wall City," "Wall Countries," "Wall World."

Right here, two towers rose up to touch the heavens, but before that there was a wooden stockade to protect our Dutch ancestors from Algonquins, bears, and wolves. Built in 1653, the city wall was regularly dismantled by the residents, who used the logs and the posts to buttress or heat their houses with their tiled gable roofs. Under my feet, in New Amsterdam, the World Trade Center has joined the ruins of colonial buildings, the wine pitchers, the bricks, the glass and nails of centuries gone by, the fields of wheat, barley, and tobacco, the remains of the pigs that gamboled through the dark streets of hovels, and the bones of sheep and men who came from the other side of the world to this land. Long, long ago, Indians planted rye here where the World Trade Center once stood.

10:01

THE RESCUE SERVICES REACHED US. YOU NEVER SAW US ON TV. Nobody took photos of us. All you know of us are disheveled figures scrambling down the walls, bodies hurled into the void, arms waving white tablecloths in the ether like scraps of cloud. The thunderous noise of the falls in the documentary by the Naudet brothers. The only film about the tragedy is the work of two Frenchmen.

But they didn't show the falling limbs, the fountains of blood, the melded sections of steel, flesh, and plastic. You didn't smell the burning electrical cables, the whiff of a short circuit amplified by 100,000 volts. You didn't hear the animal cries, like pigs with their throats cut, like calves torn limb from limb; only these were not calves, but minds capable of pleading.

I'm sorry? Decency? Important not to upset children? Morally wrong to turn victims' suffering into tabloid television? Offensive to the families of the victims? It's not as if we use kid gloves when the carnage takes place overseas. Plane crashes are routinely photographed and the images sold everywhere but in New York. Journalists—especially American journalists—are not much bothered by so-called "respect for the families." What? This carnage of human flesh is disgusting? It's reality that is disgusting—and refusing to look at it, more so. Why did you see no pictures of our dislocated legs and arms, our severed torsos, our spilled entrails? Why did the dead go unseen? It was not some ethical code of practice; it was self-censorship, maybe just censorship, period. Five minutes after the first plane crashed into our tower, the tragedy was already a hostage to fortune in a media war. And patriotism? Of course. Knee-jerk patriotism made the American press swagger about, censor our suffering, edit out shots of the jumpers, the photographs of those burn victims, the body parts. You could call it a spontaneous *omertà*, a media blackout unprecedented since the first Gulf War. I'm not sure that all of the victims would consent to be expunged in this manner. I would have liked us to be shown for all the world to see. People should have the courage to look at us, just as we force ourselves to witness the images in Alain Resnais's World War II documentary *Nuit et Brouillard*. But already it was war; in time of war, you hush up the damage done by the enemy. It's important to put up a good show, it's part of the propaganda. The victims were hugely compensated. Mary is rich now, what with my life insurance, the relief fund, Social Security contributions, and the boys' inheritance. Candace will get nothing. Candace will have to do a lot more lingerie photo shoots. And it was thus that one of the greatest postwar campaigns of media disinformation was perpetrated. Don't show the blood, I can't bear to look at it. When a building collapses, feel free to repeat the footage endlessly. But whatever you do, don't show what was inside: our bodies.

10:02

THE AIR PIRATES LIVED COMFORTABLY IN FLORIDA IN SMALL SEASIDE resorts with beaches and shopping malls. I need someone to explain this to me. One day, someone will have to explain to me how fifteen young, westernized Saudi graduates in suits, whose families lived in Germany and later in America—guys who drank wine, watched TV, drove cars and flight simulators, ate at Pizza Hut, occasionally visited prostitutes and sex shops—how men like this could slit stewardesses' throats with a craft knife (you have to hold the girl with one hand—a stewardess wriggles a lot, shrieks, loud piercing screams, you have to press the blade hard against the carotid and the trachea, pierce the skin, cutting the nerves; blood spurts everywhere; she struggles, kicking her heels into your shins, digging her elbow into your solar plexus . . . no, it's not an easy thing to do), how these guys could take control of four Boeings only to destroy them by flying them into buildings in the name of Allah. I'm quite prepared to accept that Allah is great, but even so . . . Documentary filmmaker Claude Lanzmann says that the Shoah is a mystery: September 11 is too. Were they on drugs, and if so, what? Coke, speed, alcohol, hash, EPO, Belgian skunk? Had they been promised something other than the thousand virgin sluts of Paradise? Hard cash for their next of kin? And how many of those in the unit knew about the suicidal nature of the mission?

When I was little, Jacques Martin used to present a show on Antenne 2 called *Incredible but True*. You'd see him haranguing pensioners bussed in to the Théâtre de l'Empire.

"Incredible but . . ."

And in unison, they'd all chime in:

" . . . TRUE!"

I think he could have done a special edition on September 11. It was an event which was unforeseeable because it was impossible. It is, quite literally, incomprehensible, by which I mean it passes human understanding. Who are these men capable of such a thing? Who are Mohammed Atta, Abdulaziz Alomari, Marwan Alshehhi and their buddies?

Are they (check box as applicable)

- Towel-head fundamentalists? ❐
- Psychotic madmen? ❐
- Neo-fascists? ❐
- Saints in turbans? ❐
- Morons manipulated by a billionaire who is an ex-CIA agent? ❐
- Heroes of the exploited third world? ❐
- Hardcore post-punks drugged up to the eyeballs? ❐
- Camel-fuckers who need to be napalmed pronto? ❐
- Depressed nihilists? ❐
- Militant anti-globalization activists? ❐
- Kamikazes? (c'mon now, all together!) ❐
- Incredible but . . . TRUE? ❐

10:03

I MADE TWO MISTAKES:

1. having children;
2. bringing them here for breakfast.

I'm starting to see things differently. As if they're not happening now, as if they're already memories. It's strange observing everything from this distance, which confers on it a sense of imminent self-destruction. The world is so much more beautiful when you're no longer really a part of it. I know that I'll remember even when I no longer have a memory. Because, even after death, others will remember for us.

10:04

THE "KILLER CLOUD," A TORNADO OF RUBBLE, 100-FOOT STEEL girders like train tracks falling from the sky, sheets of glass 100 feet square, sharp as giant razor blades, the killer cloud moved like a tidal wave at 50 miles an hour through the alleys onto Fulton Street, and this, too, is an image lifted from disaster movies: we've seen this same scene in *The Blob, Godzilla*, *Independence Day*, *Armageddon*, in *Die Hard 2* and in *Deep Impact*: that morning, reality contented itself with imitating special effects. Some bystanders didn't run for cover, so convinced were they that they'd seen it all before.

10:05

ONE LAST TIME, THE TELEPHONE MANAGES TO GET THROUGH. IT IS Mary in tears. I didn't try to reassure her.

"We're not going to make it out of here. Pray for us."

"Couldn't you have used the stairs?"

"There's no way out, no rescue services. Please, you have to believe me, don't ask any more questions, I swear I've done everything I possibly could. Keep calling 911. Tell them to open the door to the roof."

"WAIT! Don't hang up! Please, PLEASE!"

The line went dead. The building roared like a wounded dinosaur, like King Kong at the end of the movie. Laughing, I tossed bundles of money out the window. Nothing but hundred-dollar bills. Must have been about five or six thousand bucks, whipped away by the wind. And everyone laughed, a frantic laughter, a liberating fit of the giggles that began with me and pealed around me on the top floor of the glass penitentiary.

10:06

THE MORNING AFTER THE TERRORIST ATTACKS, AMERICAN FLAGS blossomed throughout the megalopolis. One year on, they have wilted. Has the tide of nationalism been stemmed? No: fear has returned, it's important to do nothing to attract the attention of an eventual enemy. Too many people are allergic to the stars and stripes, no point getting them riled up. The United States of America continues to account for 40 percent of global defense expenditure. I've been wondering for some days now what it is about New York that has changed. I've just worked it out: America has just discovered doubt. They never knew René Descartes. Freud brought them a plague, but the land of my forefathers, the land of milk and honey, had never experienced doubt. And now, whichever way I turn, I see doubt being sown in the American dream. Not only in the people. Cars doubt. Supermarkets doubt. Parking lots aren't sure of anything anymore. Deconsecrated churches transformed into nightclubs doubt themselves. Traffic jams are no longer convinced of their certainty. Designer stores wonder whether it's all worth it. Traffic lights don't stay red for long. Billboard ads feel ashamed. Airplanes are frightened of frightening people. Buildings put the past behind them. America has entered the age of Descartes.

10:07

THE WOMEN HAD WON: NO ONE WANTED TO GROW OLD WITH them anymore.

I spent so much time jerking off that in the end I got a hard-on just looking at a box of Kleenex. I was a 40-year-old single man. I had orgasms nonstop. I thought this was freedom, but no; it was loneliness. I had given up on love. I had chosen pleasure over happiness. Couples depressed me. I saw married men as eunuchs and prisoners. I thought: you're not a man unless you fuck a different woman every day.

I was incapable of living for anyone but myself.

10:08

On September 11, 2001, a branch of Burger King was transformed into a morgue. Brooks Brothers looked as though it had been whitewashed. Towering over Pier A, two colossal Apple billboards illustrated with photos of Franklin and Eleanor Roosevelt bore the slogan THINK DIFFERENT (Roosevelt was president of the United States when Pearl Harbor happened, but that's a coincidence). On West Street, they laid torn sheets over the dismembered bodies but the ground was still strewn with bare flesh. "I saw a whole heart stuck to one of the mezzanine windows. Arms, legs, guts, severed bodies, human organs all over the plaza. I couldn't stop thinking: it's not real, it's a film. It can't be real. I couldn't bring myself to look at it." (Testimony of Medhi Dadgarian, a survivor from the 72nd floor). Everything below 14th Street was cordoned off. In all of Lower Manhattan, there was neither electricity nor gas. At the foot of the Twin Towers they found pieces of Rodin sculptures, bronze bodies mingled with broken human corpses. Beneath the rubble, hundreds of pagers bleeped in the jackets of crushed firefighters. Beneath Ground Zero: a subway station in darkness, the ceiling ripped open by the debris, girders twisted, concrete powdered. A newspaper kiosk beneath the fine white powder, charred cables hanging above the magazines and the candy bars. A gaping trench running diagonally across WTC Plaza, where the scattered columns of the towers looked like branches of trees ripped off by a hurricane. New Yorkers of every age, creed, race, and social class waited patiently in a line that stretched for four blocks just to make an appointment to donate blood.

The Earth slumps under the weight of rubble like a ballroom on the morning after a party. Things need to be tidied up, but no one knows where to start. Faced with the enormity of the task, we sigh, empty an ashtray; the champagne has gone flat. The windows of the world are dark, their eyes gouged out. It might have been funny, before, while the night laughed. Now the streets are cold, the people hurrying. They are running because they are afraid to stop. They can no longer remember why they are so determined to be rich. A car glides between the towers like a toy on an electric circuit. On the sidewalk, we act as if we had not all been seriously injured. All convalescing.

From here, we can penetrate the unspeakable, the inexpressible. Please excuse our misuse of ellipsis. I have cut out the awful descriptions. I have not done so out of propriety, nor out of respect for the victims, because I believe that describing their slow agonies, their ordeal, is also a mark of respect. I cut them because, in my opinion, it is more appalling still to allow you to imagine what became of them.

10:09

I WOULD SO LIKE IT TO BE YESTERDAY. TO GO BACK TO JUST BEFORE. If I had to do it all again, I wouldn't. "Oh, I believe in yesterday" (a Beatles song).

The helicopters flew past us, watched us dying.

"The only thing I can do now is pray to God that nothing like this ever happens again."

When you were born, I cried with joy just looking at you.

"Dad," says David, who is very pale, "I've got a pain in my tummy. Can you call the doctor?"

"Don't worry, sweetheart, he's on his way."

He had 40 percent burns to his stomach.

"I'm tired . . . can I go sleep?"

"NO! David, listen to Daddy! David?"

"You can wake me up when the galaxy has been saved."

10:10

In Windows on the World, the customers were gassed, burned and reduced to ash. To them, as to so many others, we owe a duty of memory.

10:11

Death of David Yorston (1994–2001)

> A child in himself, changed by eternity
>
> —Edgar Allan Poe

10:12

It is at this point that I whip out another of my famous ITNNOTs (Instant Though Not Necessarily Original Theories). This hatred that America inspires is love. Someone who despises you so much is someone who wants your attention, consequently someone who subconsciously loves you. Bin Laden does not realize it, but he worships America and wants to be admired by it. He would not make so much effort if he did not want America to look at him.

Who is mad? Who is sacred? Our God is crucified. We worship a bearded man in a loincloth tortured on a cross. It is time to found a new religion whose symbol would be two towers ablaze. Let us build churches of parallel parallelepipeds in which, at the moment of communion, two remote-controlled scale models of planes would be crashed. At the moment when the planes pierce the towers, the congregation would be asked to kneel.

10:13

LIBERALISM HAS NOTHING TO DO WITH MORALITY. THE MOTTO OF the French Republic should apply to the whole world: Freedom, Equality, Brotherhood. The problem is that this human principle is an inhuman falsehood.

The West booms that we must be free! Free! Shout from the rooftops how free we are, brag about how free we are. Die to defend that freedom. All well and good. But I am not happy when I am free. I've studied the problem from every angle but in vain. In spite of my Texan insincerity, now that it's too late to go back, I'm forced to admit it. I liked Mary better in my dad's car, her slender fingers and her nails and the smell of flowers everywhere and the twilight round her eyes. Moments gleaned until the last moment. I liked Jerry better when he was born, his repulsive, swollen, blue head, oh my God, I'm going to have to take care of this filthy thing my whole life, and then he opens his eyes and smiles. I liked it better having Candace hold me in her arms, so that I could forget the terror of being me.

I wasn't happy when I was free.

10:14

I'm on a plain / I can't complain.

—Nirvana

In his *History of French Literature* (1936), Albert Thibaudet explains that a generation is an age group who, at twenty, lived through a historic event from which they will never recover and which will forever mark them. In his own case (Thibaudet was born in 1874), it was the Dreyfus affair. For the succeeding generations there were the two world wars, the war in Algeria, then May 1968. My parents' generation was irrevocably marked by 1968. Their society was turned upside down: morals changed and with them behavior. Nothing was ever as it had been before: the way people dressed, the way they spoke, customs, education. Everything they had been taught was no longer of any use to them. For my parents, 1968 was like being born again, hence their inevitable divorce. They no longer had any reference points, their parents were squares, they didn't understand their religion anymore, didn't know how to talk to them. How can you expect to stay with someone when everything is disintegrating? For my generation, it was 1989: I was 25, and the fall of the Berlin Wall sounded the death knell of ideologies. A reckless hope was born: liberalism would conquer the whole planet. So I got a job in advertising, the military wing of capitalism. I pulled through, but that's another story, one I've already told. Like all the writers of my generation, I was forever marked by the eighties religion of money, hypnotized by the glamour, the arrogance of yuppies, synthesizer music and designer furniture, fashion shows and the democratization of porn, the taste for discotheques and the poetry of airports. That's how it goes: my generation is the generation of François Mitterand and *Globe* magazine, which saw the left embrace realism and abandon utopias. My generation despises May '68 because all generations have a duty to destroy the one that came before. My generation will remain forever traumatized by the death of communism, by supermodels and cocaine. The generation that followed, those born in the 1980s, which will destroy my own, was twenty on September 11, 2001. In their eyes, I am the living embodiment of jet-set superficiality, of the entryist paradox, media corruption, and self-important vacuousness. I wonder how they will survive the World Trade Center: can they grow up in the smoldering ruins of materialism? What will they build in the place of the global shopping mall? What will their dreams be made of, other than molten steel and charred entrails? How can they build on the ruins of my generation, the destruction of the seventies and the failure of the eighties, the breakdown of the designer-label society? What will it see from its window on the world? Did the creed of comfort and consumption and therefore of money as the sole hope truly die in New York in 2001?

Our future has vanished. Our future is the past tense.

10:15

THE TWO TRADERS ARE IN THE CONFERENCE ROOM. THEY KNOW it's all over; they're up to their thighs in water, but it is the smoke that is drowning them. Chairs overturned, purple corpses around them, those of suffocated colleagues and bosses.

They clambered onto the oval, ebony, 30-foot conference table. He dropped his pants and she took off her blouse. Their bodies are salon tanned; despite the stench of death and the unbearable heat, it's really hot to watch them.

"I'm dying of happiness," says the blonde in Ralph Lauren. "I'm dying loving you."

"Death is better than Viagra," says the guy in Kenneth Cole. "You were my reason for living; you're my reason for dying."

In heaven, there were no thousand virgins, but there were once two. It's not only in hell that passions blaze.

10:16

F. SCOTT FITZGERALD'S NOTEBOOKS HAVE RECENTLY BEEN TRANSlated into French. I discovered the title he almost gave *The Great Gatsby*:

AMONG THE ASH HEAPS AND MILLIONAIRES

I'm scared of dying. I'm proud of my spinelessness. My complete lack of physical courage forces me to live under the permanent protection of the police and the law. My complete lack of physical courage is what distinguishes me from an animal.

It's easy to be dead in the future. It's more difficult to be dead in the present. You have to go on living right up to the moment when you're no longer living. Say "Merci," never forgetting that in English "merci" is mercy. You've got no time to have the last rites or to think up a brilliant epitaph, some stylish last words to issue with your last breath, for posterity. When death takes you by surprise, is there a posterity?

10:17

A FAT LOT OF GOOD COMPASSION IS TO ME. BY DINT OF BEING SO compassionate, Judeo-Christian democracies are easy to crush. That's what the aerial assassins set out to prove. Nobody among the tender, charitable, liberal Judeo-Christians is safe anymore. They wanted the nice, privileged people to know what it feels like to Hate. Like Robert Mitchum's fingers in *The Night of the Hunter*: LOVE HATE. Hate is love.

Jesus turned the other cheek—okay, Jesus wasn't violent. But he felt hatred, even if he rejected it, even if he did not admit it, it was within him, the implacable thirst for justice. And on the Cross he bawled everyone out and denied his father. Jesus on the Cross didn't give a toss about compassion.

10:18

FAR FROM YOU, MY HEART SHATTERED LIKE A WINDOW.

The Mercer Hotel, designed by a Frenchman (Christian Liaigre), is situated downtown in Soho, a few blocks from the World Trade Center, but I've arrived a year too late. The new mayor of New York, Michael Bloomberg, who owns a television station like Silvio Berlusconi in Italy, set himself two objectives: get rid of cigarette smokers and noise pollution. His predecessor had succeeded in getting the whores off 42nd Street and the tramps out of the Village. Soon, Gotham City will be one big pristine shopping mall. An island trade center. You're not permitted to smoke in bars, in restaurants, not even in nightclubs. Sometimes, you're not permitted to dance! Babylonian sensualists are an endangered minority. This obsession with tranquillity and cleanliness seems like an instinctive response to the lessons of purity and virtue of Islamic fundamentalists, those bearded hypocrites. It betrays the terror of a metropolis in danger. When democracy is threatened, Manhattan becomes . . . Switzerland.

* * *

I no longer leave the Mercer. I live there like a recluse, like singer-songwriter Michel Polnareff at the Royal Monceau. I have lunch and dinner in the Mercer Kitchen on the ground floor. At 10:18 P.M., I drink my vodka-cranberry at the Submercer, the hotel nightclub. I live in autarchy in the most fashionable building in New York as if I was living in a family *pensione* in Tuscany. The porter and the receptionist smile at me pityingly and wonder whether this melancholy Frenchman will have the wherewithal to pay his bill at the end of his stay. The celebrities who hang out in the hotel bar (Benicio Del Toro, Amanda de Cadenet) can't work out why this guy with the beard sits alone humming Cat Stevens songs, jotting down their every word, their every move in his little black notebook. Methodically, I drink myself into a stupor, slumped on a designer sofa, talking to no one, often crying, thinking of you, missing you.

10:19

THEY WANT US TO FEEL GUILTY. BUT GUILTY FOR WHAT? I'M NOT responsible for what my country did when it was growing up. Black slavery, the genocide of the Indians, raging liberalism, it wasn't me, guys, I came along much later! All I did was be born here, in the Big Guy's house, but I'm not one of them. The only thing I control is my real estate office. Okay, I sold apartments for more than they were worth. I've got to admit all realtors are crooks: they sell you something you'll never own. Don't you understand that here on earth you'll never own anything? That we're all tenants? I sold the wind, some temporary square footage you'd have to slave all your life to pay off. Average American debt is 110 percent of annual salary: a world record. The funniest thing about it is that it's the young who congratulate themselves that they're not paying rent anymore but go on making interest payments every month. What's the difference? A realtor is a man who forces other men to work to pay off something they're still renting, since a homeowner is just a tenant trapped in his property, a debtor who can't move house.

Okay, so I'm not innocent, but I'm not a criminal either. I

didn't deserve to be executed. I don't know whether I am the embodiment of Good, but I never wished Evil on anyone. I've sinned, cheated on Mary, divorced, abandoned Jerry and David; okay, so I'm far from perfect, but since when do they burn people alive for that? What could I do if Guatemalan kids were working fifteen hours a day for slave wages to do the job for me? And I wasn't even born when Hiroshima and Nagasaki happened, for God's sake! Fuck, in what sense am I complicit in what goes on in Palestinian refugee camps with all those swarthy guys throwing rocks at tanks and suicide-bombing themselves all day long instead of going to work like everyone else? I mean, shit, it's miles away and we haven't got a clue what it's about. Hairy bearded sand-eaters, crouching round in sandals with a machine gun in one hand shouting slogans that are as hateful as they are incomprehensible. There's too much dust in those countries, and they die from the heat; it's annoying to be so hot first thing in the morning when you're eating insects for breakfast, you're dying of thirst; in the end, either you go and lie down or you top yourself and take everybody else with you.

Who's behind the attack? Arafat? The Unabomber? You might say, what difference does it make whether you're murdered by Bin Laden or Timothy McVeigh, Al Qaeda or the Ku Klux Klan? Frankly, my dear, I don't give a Saddam! Violence is part of man's nature. In theory, culture, religion, society, civilization are supposed to subdue it. In theory. Have pity on us. Oh Lord, take pity on Jerry, on David, on Carthew Yorston of Austin, Texas. Have mercy on us. What about Arabic—how do you say "mercy" in Arabic?

10:20

A port is a charming sojourn for a soul worn out by the struggles of life. The amplitude of the sky, the mobile architecture of the clouds, the changing colors of the sea, the sparkling of the beacons, are all a prism marvelously suited to amusing the eyes without ever wearying them. The slender forms of the ships, with their complicated rigging, upon which the swell of the sea imprints harmonious oscillations, serve to preserve in the soul a taste for rhythm and beauty. And then, above all else, there is a sort of mysterious and aristocratic pleasure, for him who has neither curiosity nor ambition, in contemplating, while lying on the belvedere or leaning his elbows against the pier, all of the movements of those who leave and those who return, of those who still have strength of will, the desire to travel, or to enrich themselves.

—Charles Baudelaire, *Paris Spleen,* 1865.
It should be retitled *New York Spleen.*

10:21

SINCE DAVID DIED, JERRY WON'T LET GO OF HIM, CRIES ON HIS COLD forehead, strokes his closed eyelids. I stand up, take him in my arms, a little prince with blond, lifeless hair. Jerry reads my thoughts; he shudders with grief. I'm tired of playing the hero. Like the receptionist said: not trained for that. Jerry's hand tightens on my arm; in the other, he holds David's limp hand, which dangles, swinging in the void. I hug this beloved flesh to my smoke-blackened shirt, his little face black like the time he used matches to burn a cork to make Indian war paint, summer 1997, Yosemite National Park. I wish I could stop remembering, my heart is bursting. C'mon, c'mon kids, let's get out of here, let's do what we should have done long ago, beat it, hit the road again, *adiós amigos, hasta la vista,* baby, the glass is broken, look through the Windows on the World, look, Jerry, freedom, no, Jerry my little hero, don't look down, keep your blue eyes fixed on the horizon, New York harbor, the ballet of helpless helicopters, you never saw *Apocalypse Now*, you were so young, how could those murderers, c'mon darling, come on, my little lambs, Space Mountain will be like cat's piss compared to this, hold on tight to me, Jerry, I love you, come with Daddy, we're going home, we're taking your little brother home, come and surf the clouds of fire, you were my angels and nothing will ever split us up again, heaven is being with you, take a deep breath and if you're scared, all you've gotta do is close your eyes. We know what self-sacrifice is too.

Just before we jump, Jerry looks me straight in the eyes. What was left of his face twisted one last time. It wasn't just a nosebleed anymore.

"Will Mom be sad?"

"Don't think about that. We have to be strong. I love you, honey. You're a hell of a kid."

"I love you too, Dad. Hey, Dad, you know what? I'm not scared of falling—I'm not crying and neither are you."

"I've never known anyone as brave as you, Jerry. Never. You ready, buddy? On three . . ."

"One, two . . . three!"

Our mouths gradually distorted from the speed. The wind made us make curious faces. I can still hear Jerry laughing, holding tight to my hand and to his little brother's, plummeting through the heavens. Thank you for that last laugh, O Lord, thank you for Jerry's laugh. For a split second, I really believed we were flying.

10:22

STEFAN ZWEIG WROTE: "UNCONSCIOUSLY, NEW YORK MIMICS THE mountains, the sea, and the rivers," and Céline speaks of a "standing city" because he never saw the World Trade Center lie down.

The Americans walked on the moon, but on the days that followed September 11, 2001, there was no need to go so far: New York had become a dead planet. A carpet of white dust covered the asphalt. All that remained of a 110-story building were two metal girders, twisted like fingers clawing at the sky. Like a crushed space module. The silence pierced by police sirens. In America, everything is bigger, even terrorist attacks. In France, a Métro station blows up, a clothing store is destroyed, but the buildings remain more or less vertical. Here, this foreign terrorist attack is instantly the most murderous in western history: the greatest number of civilians massacred in one fell swoop since the founding of the United States.

I had planned a chapter here called "Death: A User's Manual." As if Georges Perec had exchanged 11, rue Simon-Crubellier for the square bordered by Vesey, Liberty, West, and Church Streets. By now I'm in too much of a hurry to get home; I want to eat my wedding cake; I want to snuggle up to you, if you'll have me.

I look up and give a knowing wink to Carthew, Jerry, and David, who may be looking down on me through the gray winter fog. The sea carries off the sound of the sirens, of the gulls, of the cranes and the tourist helicopters. New York in black and white, granite and marble, annihilated, disappears in the mist suspended from the steel pylons. Even so, I'm alive. No need to make a mountain out of a molehill.

10:23

SOMETIMES I DREAM OF A HEAP OF THOUSANDS OF TONS OF SMOLdering bodies and melted steel in which are fused man and stone, computers and severed arms, elevators and charred legs, believers and atheists, fire and the sword. . . . And then it passes. And then it returns: I see walls with eyes embedded in them, heads split open by glass, bodies broken on fax machines, brains trickling onto photocopiers. God created this too. And I dream that I'm floating, with my two children in my arms over a mountain of rubble. And perhaps I'm not dreaming. Perhaps we're floating over WTC plaza, forever windswept, emptier still now the towers are gone. Now, they call it "the site," and give guided tours. The wind still blows, between zero and the infinite. We are within it, we are the wind.

Once, in this place, man built two towers on this earth. "Rest in Peace": here we rest in war. Only death can make us immortal. We are not dead: we are prisoners of the sun or of the snow. Broken rays of sunlight dart between the snowflakes, which fall in slow motion like a rain of confetti. Shards of glass apparently migrate beneath the skin. Put some glass in your veins. Do this in memory of me. I died for you and you and you and you and you and you and you and you.

10:24

I TRULY DON'T KNOW WHY I WROTE THIS BOOK. PERHAPS BECAUSE I couldn't see the point of speaking of anything else. What else is there to write? The only interesting subjects are those that are taboo. We must write what is forbidden. French literature is a long history of disobedience. Nowadays, books must go where television does not. Show the invisible, speak the unspeakable. It may be impossible, but that is its raison d'être. Literature is a *Mission: Impossible.*

The singular interest of living in a democracy is to criticize it. In fact, this is how we know we are living in a democracy. One cannot criticize a dictatorship. Even when it is attacked, threatened, scorned, democracy must prove that it is democratic by speaking ill of democracy.

In saying that, I realize that I'm not being honest. I am also obliged to concede that in leaning on the first great hyperterrorist attack, my prose takes on a power it would not otherwise have. This novel uses tragedy as a literary crutch.

There is another reason. My American genealogy goes back to the "patriot" Amos Wheeler, hero of the American Revolution, born in Pepperell, Massachusetts in 1741, died in Cambridge, Massachusetts on June 21, 1775, from a wound to the thigh sustained at the battle of Bunker Hill five days earlier. His name appears on the Bunker Hill monument as well as on the monument in Washington, D.C. A posthumous son was born a month later, in July 1775: Amos Wheeler II. His daughter, Olive Wheeler, married a man named Jobe Knight and gave him a son, Eldorado Knight, who married Frances Matilda Harben, whose daughter Nellie Harben Knight was the mother of Grace Carthew Yorstoun, my paternal grandmother. I'm an eighth generation descendant of patriot Amos Wheeler, born 228 years after his death. Grace Carthew Yorstoun married Charles Beigbeder, my father's father. She moved to France, gained 110 pounds from eating foie gras, and died in Pau in the Béarn having given birth to two daughters and two sons (among them, my father), all this without ever losing the Yankee accent that made the Rotary Club members of Pyrénées-Atlantique smile.

If you go back eight generations, all white Americans are Europeans. We are the same: even if we are not all Americans, our problems are theirs, and theirs are ours.

10:25

THAT MORNING, WE WERE AT THE TOP OF THE WORLD, AND I WAS the center of the universe.

I was right to tell Jerry and David that we were on an imaginary theme park ride: now, there are guided tours of Ground Zero. It has become a tourist attraction, like the Statue of Liberty, which we will never get to visit. Tickets for the WTC site are available from the Seaport; they're free. There is a long line to climb a wooden podium that overlooks the desolate esplanade. The guide hurries the voyeurs. But there's nothing to see except an immense expanse of concrete, a parking lot with no cars, the biggest tombstone in the world. The night blushes with embarrassment at times to think of it; the surrounding buildings refuse to twinkle. And the darkness keeps us warm. The river is violet and blue; seen from above it's very beautiful.

We've become a tourist attraction. See, kids? It's us they're coming to see now.

10:26

AT NOCHE (THE NEW RESTAURANT OPENED BY WINDOWS ON THE World owner David Emil on Times Square), I collar one of the former employees of Windows.

"I'm a French writer and I'm currently working on a novel about your old restaurant."

"Why?"

"Because my grandmother was American—her name was Grace Carthew Yorstoun, and I didn't go to her funeral. I was in Switzerland with my father and my brother when we got the news. I preferred to ski; the weather was beautiful, my father was on pretty bad terms with his brother—we didn't go to Pau."

"I'm sorry, sir, but I don't understand what you're talking about."

"I never really knew her. Her name was Grace, like Grace Kelly, but we called her Granny. She was from one of the grand old families of the American South. At the end of her life, she looked like Mr. Magoo. You see my chin? I get that from her."

"Listen, I've got work to do. And I don't care about your grandmother. You're bothering me, mister!"

"She was a descendant of John Adams, the second president of the United States. I've got cousins, the Harbens, in Dallas. I haven't seen them for twenty-five years. They told me I'm also descended from a famous fur trapper: Daniel Boone."

"So what?"

"We do not hate you. You scare us because you rule the world. But we're blood relations. France helped your country to be born. Later, you liberated us. And my cousin died in your restaurant on September 11, 2001, with his two sons."

I don't know why I lied like that. I wanted to move him. Cowardice makes you a pathological liar. Carthew Yorstoun was my grandmother's family name. Take out a "u" and you have Carthew Yorston, a fictional character.

"Excuse me, but I'm so sick and tired of Nine-Eleven . . ."

"Don't worry, I'm going, I don't want to bother you. Just one question: do you know the Dionne Warwick song?"

"Of course."

And there we are, two citizens of planet earth, humming "The windows of the world are covered with rain," at first we feel like fools, the customers think we're drunk, we don't sing very loudly, then the chorus comes and we are howling like piglets, like tramps, like brothers.

10:27

THERE'S NOTHING TO UNDERSTAND, MY LITTLE GHOSTS WITH YOUR delicate little hands. We died for nothing. The collapse of the North Tower will occur in one minute (a tremor of eight seconds registering 2.3 on the Richter scale) but we won't see it because we're no longer on board. In the smoke and the rubble, the TV antenna remains vertical as it falls before tilting slightly to the left. The spire sank into the smoke like the ship's mast into the ocean spray. Tower No. 1 took ten seconds to completely collapse, straight as a rocket ready for taking off with the film running backward. Remember us, please. We three are the burning phoenix which will rise from its ashes. Phoenix isn't only in Arizona.

10:28

At night, the avenues of New York are rivers of diamonds. At night, in this city, it is not night. Convinced I am unique, I walk down the West Side Highway at 10:28 P.M. as if walking on stage to accept an Oscar. Death wanted none of me in New York. The current situation in the West is often compared to the fall of the Roman Empire. Am I decadent? I don't think so. My lifestyle is suicidal, not me. I'm just a nihilist who doesn't want to die. Night falls over the Site: a clearing in a forest of glass. A year and a half after the tragedy, all that remains of the World Trade Center is a wasteland, a gray plateau surrounded by a wire fence. I will never know if what took place is as I imagined, nor will you. A siren in the night: the blaring ricochets in the narrow streets. White smoke rises from the drain between a Cadillac FOR SALE and the cracked sidewalk. The same smoke, ever-present in the past—we look at it differently now. A dead world, haunted by pretzel vendors. Not far from the Holocaust Memorial (18 First Place, south of Battery Park City), I looked up: music sneaks out of an apartment and women's laughter, the tinkle of ice in glasses and the yellow glow of American parties. I know this song: a global hit ("Shine on Me" by the Praise Cats, with a demented rhythmic piano and crazy lyrics like all disco hits: "I've got peace deep in my soul, I've got love making me whole / Since you opened up your heart and shined on me"). I suddenly felt an incredible burst of joy, the same burst of gratitude that I felt on August 29, 1999, when I held you in my arms and welcomed you to Earth. I play with the little blue Tiffany box in my pocket with the engagement ring inside. The foghorn is silent now. Only the melody *dong dong dong tzing tzing tzing* drifts from the window like a stream of warm air lifts flimsy summer curtains, the rest is silence. I mumble the words like a psalm. "I've got peace deep in my soul, I've got love making me whole." I'm ashamed of my Catholic joy. Obscene in front of the largest crematorium in the world. Obscenely, inexplicably happy to be alive simply because I'm thinking about the people I love. Planes smash into walls and our society with them. We are kamikazes who want to live. Love alone gives me the right to hope. Freighters pass in the darkness—red lights like a nautical airport gliding across the black mirror. Birds fly off toward the dead stars. I pass the Cunard Building, where, a century before, people bought their tickets to travel on the *Titanic*. The mouth of the contaminated river meets the sky. We flirt constantly with oblivion, death is our sister, it is possible to love, no doubt our happiness is hidden somewhere in that chaos. Will there be a worldwide democracy in thirty years' time? In thirty years I and the rest of the planet will be forcibly disillusioned, but I don't care, because in thirty years, I'll be seventy. Somewhere, far off on the sea, the moon will soon be reflected and the water will look like a dance floor or a tombstone. I am sorry to be alive but my time will come. My time will come.

10:29

THE PLANE THAT WAS TAKING ME BACK TO PARIS, CLEAVING THE clouds with its shark's-fin aileron, doesn't fly anymore. Sitting in an armchair at 1,250 miles per hour over this fathomless ocean, I was crossing the clouds to come back and ask you for your hand. I could feel life coursing through my veins like an electric current. I got up to stretch my legs, leaned forward, and then I had an idea. I lay down on the floor, on the carpet in the aisle, fists clenched stretched toward the cockpit. The stewardess smiled, convinced I was doing some stretching exercise. And do you know what I thought? That if I just closed my eyes and took away the cabin, the engines and all the other passengers, I'd be alone in the ether, 30,000 feet up, speeding through the blue at supersonic speed. Yes, I thought I was a superhero.

Paris–New York City, 2002–2003

Acknowledgments

Thanks to Bruce Springsteen for his latest album, and also to Suicide, Robbie Williams, Sigur Ros, the White Stripes, Richard Ashcroft, Zwan and of course thanks to Cat Stevens–Yussuf Islam for his boxed set: *In Search of the Center of the Universe* (A&M Records).

Thanks to Amélie Labrande for becoming Amélie Beigbeder.

Thanks to Emmanuel Auboyneau for the financial jargon, to Francisca Matteoli for the photo of Windows on the World, and to René Guitton for the two towers of Babel.

Thanks to the *New York Times* (article "120 Minutes: Last Words at the Trade Center" by Jim Dwyer, Eric Lipton, Kevin Flynn, James Glanz, and Ford Fessenden).

Thanks to the collection of eyewitness accounts compiled by Dean E. Murphy: *September 11: An Oral History* (Doubleday).

Thanks to Bruno Lavaine for the Burt Bacharach song.

To Thierry Gounaud for the cover.

And to Canal+ for the redundancy settlement.

And to Vogalène, Smecta, Lexomil, without which this book would not have seen the light of day.

Thanks to *Walk in Hemingway's Paris* by Noel Riley Fitch (St. Martin's Griffin, New York): proof that some Americans know Paris better than we do.

Thanks to Marc de Gontaut-Biron for taking me to visit Cielo, Lotus, and Taj.

Thanks to Julien Barbera for reserving the best table for me at Cipriani Downtown.

Thanks to Yann le Gallais for his champagne.

Thanks to Nicholas Bonnier for the spliff.

Thanks to David Emil and Joey du Noche.

Thanks to Concorde . . .

And long live Sean Penn!

Author's Note

A novel is a fiction; what is contained within its pages is not truth. The only way to know what took place in the restaurant on the 107th floor of the North Tower of the World Trade Center on September 11, 2001, is to invent it. Novels, I believe, are a means of understanding history; they can be windows on our world. But merging fiction with truth—and with tragedy—risks hurting those who have already suffered, something of which I was intensely aware when rereading the novel in English—the language in which the tragedy *happened.* There were, I felt, moments when it was starker and perhaps more likely to wound than I intended. Consequently some scenes have been revised for this edition.

Frédéric Beigbeder

PERMISSIONS

The publisher and author would like to thank:
Erick Miller and Andrea Love, Steve Hulme and Erick Marillo for kind permission for "Shine on Me" by the Praise Cats.

"If I Could Tell You," copyright 1945 by W. H. Auden,
from COLLECTED POEMS by W. H. Auden.
Used by permission of Random House, Inc.
"Father and Son"—Words and Music by Cat Stevens.
© 1970 Cat Music Limited. Sony Music Publishing UK.
All Rights Reserved.
"Pop Star"—Words and Music by Cat Stevens.
© 1970 Cat Music Limited. Sony Music Publishing UK.
All Rights Reserved.
"Time"—Words and Music by Cat Stevens.
© 1970 Cat Music Limited. Sony Music Publishing UK.
All Rights Reserved.
"Trouble"—Words and Music by Cat Stevens.
© 1970 Cat Music Limited. Sony Music Publishing UK.
All Rights Reserved.
"Where Do The Children Play?"—Words and Music
by Cat Stevens.
© 1970 Cat Music Limited. Sony Music Publishing UK.
All Rights Reserved.

THEME FROM NEW YORK, NEW YORK,
By: John Kander and Fred Ebb
© 1977 UNITED ARTISTS CORPORATION
All Rights Controlled By EMI Unart Catalog Inc. (Publishing) and
Warner Bros. Publications U.S. Inc. (Print)
All Rights Reserved Used by Permission
WARNER BROS. PUBLICATIONS U.S. INC., Miami, FL 33014